KOPPER

a novel

by

kp dawes

(the illustrated edition)

ISBN: 978-0-99681-251-1

For Drake and Declan

ABOUT THE AUTHOR

KP Dawes was born in Communist Poland in 1979. After escaping the country under threat of arrest the family relocated first to France and eventually the United States. KP grew up in a working-class, northwest side neighborhood of Chicago, earning degrees in Anthropology and History at Loyola University. He's been a teacher, a speechwriter, and editor. Currently he works in the publishing industry, writing books and creating art in his spare time.

Find him at **kpdawes.com**.

"What shall we do with us?"

- **Kenneth Patchen**

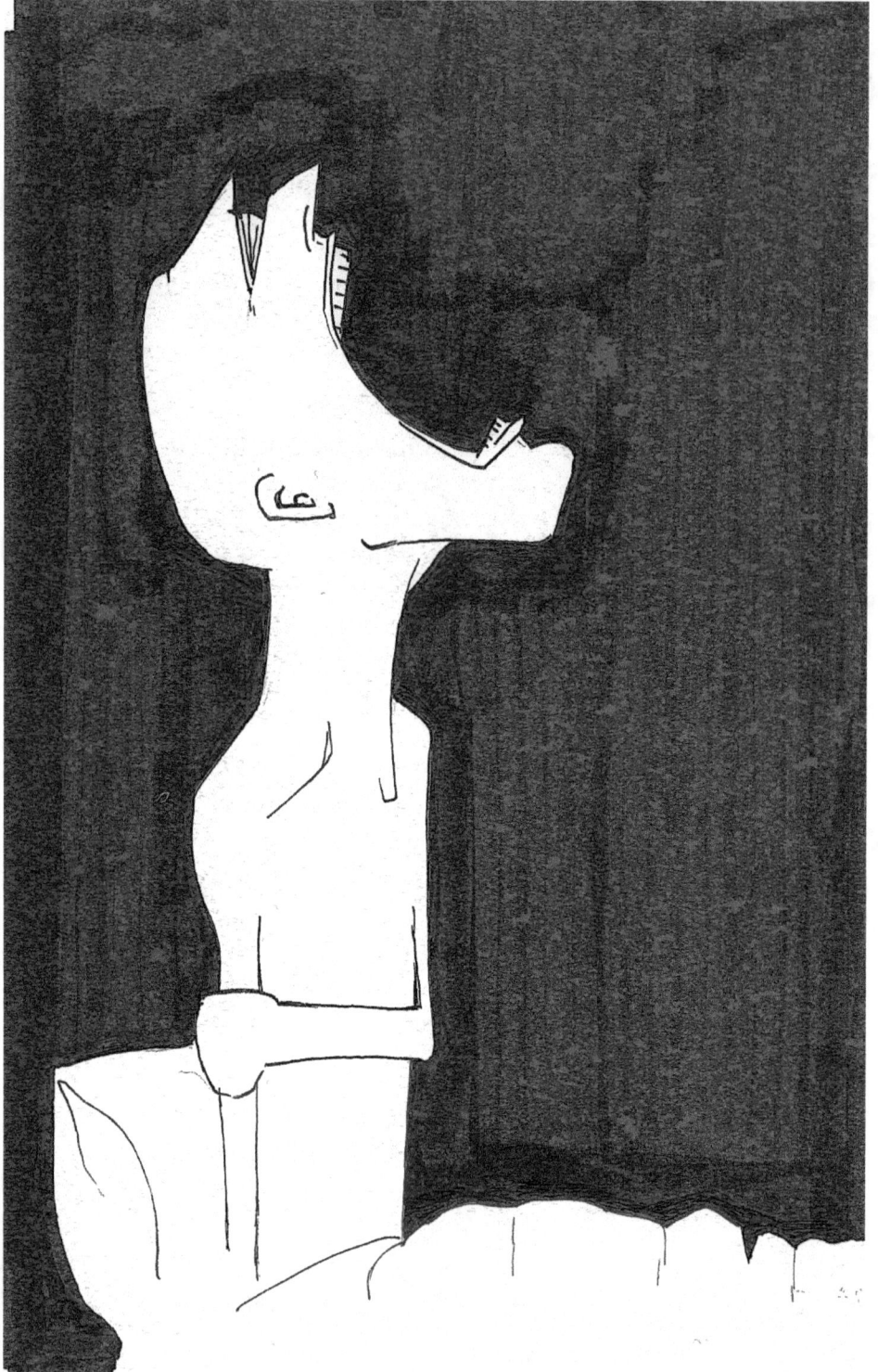

PROLOGUE

The dream was always the same. He was in his house, just as it had been when he was taken. It was a ranch house with cream-colored walls and thick wall-to-wall carpeting that would crunch when he clenched his toes.

His dad was sprawled across the couch in the living room, glasses on his face, reading one of his many history books by the light streaming from the windows. Kit couldn't make out the words on the cover but it was certainly *The Rise and Fall of the Third Reich*, or *The History of the Soviet Empire*, or *The World in the Age of Terror*. His dad read those books and then would spend all of dinner lecturing him and his little brother, reminding them how violent the world was, how dark and brutal. Then his dad would get frustrated when they wanted to talk about school, or television, or games instead. "I'm preparing you for what's out there, you should listen," he'd say.

His mom and brother were sitting at the dining room table, putting together some kind of craft project. Scraps of metal, rolls of tape, tubing, stacks of paper were everywhere. Kit couldn't tell what it was they were making and when he'd ask they'd ignore him, his brother going about cutting shapes with his scissors.

His mom loved doing crafts with them. The house was always filled with hand print turkeys, or paper hearts, or fabric flowers, depending on the season.

Kit liked doing them because his mom liked doing them. She'd hug him and kiss him and tell him how proud she was of him. He liked to see his mom happy. Invariably the praise would upset his brother. He'd grunt, pound on the table, demand to know that he'd done better. Kit didn't mind his brother, he took after their dad.

In the dream his family looked exactly like he remembered them, not aged a day in three years. Going about their business like nothing was wrong, would ever be wrong. His dad was reading his book, his mom and brother doing crafts.

Suddenly there was a loud racket from the front of the house. Without thinking Kit left his parents and brother and crossed the living room to the front door and turned the knob. Out on the front lawn were a dozen workmen, dressed in the attire of labor: hardhats, emergency vests, tool belts. They were standing around a scaffolding, shrouded in thick sheets of plastic. There were tools of every kind scattered throughout the grass and an army of generators hummed noisily off to one side. Behind them, on the sidewalk and in the street, a group of curious neighbors had gathered to watch the goings on.

Kit took a step out onto the stoop. A step onto the path leading across the sod. One more until he was at the elbow of the largest of the workmen, black skin, heavy gut in checkered shirt, grey stubble on his face. Kit pulled at the man's tool belt. Once. Twice. Three times. The workman finally glanced down, furrowed his brow and said, "You shouldn't be here. You shouldn't be here, we're not done."

"What are you building?" asked Kit.

The workman shook his head and said, "You shouldn't be here. In time. In time. Not now." And then he put a heavy mitt on Kit's shoulder and shoved him down into the grass. As Kit tried to pick himself up, Rodney Richter and Chris Caputo appeared above him, laughing. "Useless," they'd say in the same mocking tone they used every day at recess when they'd shove him against the rungs of the slide.

The dream was the same every night for three years, only the progress of the work ever changed. The project in the dining room grew more furious. The construction on the front lawn grew more complex. The shadow of the thing behind the layers of plastic grew larger.

4 kp dawes

Chapter 1: Kit

Kit didn't know why the Masters had picked him. Why of all the billions of people on his world he was the one chosen. He wasn't very big for his age. Not very strong. A mop of dark hair over dark eyes and angular, thin face. All skin and bone, or so his mom liked to tell him.

The milkwomen believed that the gods set the rolls. Hagga, his favorite, had told him exactly that when he first arrived. When he used to lay awake for days in his cell crying, crying so long and so hard that after a while only dry sobs would come and then eventually only emptiness. Now he didn't let himself cry or miss his parents, or his brother, or his home in that place called Michigan that seemed so long and far away. Bolts told him to hang on to the memory, to let it fill him and drive him to victory, but Kit seldom thought about home save for his dreams.

The grinders, Kit could never tell one from another, said that the rolls were decided by a supercomputer designed just for the purpose of selecting fighters for the games. But Kit couldn't figure what could've separated him from all the other kids on the Earth. He'd always been awkward growing up. Falling more than was natural. He liked sports well enough but not as well as other boys and certainly not as well as his brother. Above all he never liked to fight. It seemed the Masters could have picked anyone else.

"You're here, what does it matter?" said Bolts, in his heavy, raspy voice when Kit had finally summoned courage enough to ask him.

The milkwomen and the grinders weren't human, Kit noticed that on his first day, but they didn't look that different from him. The milkwomen were large and round with olive skin and hair the consistency of leather straps. The grinders were small, smaller even than him, pink and boney, and moved along hunched over with surprising speed. But neither looked otherworldly, just strange.

"The gods made us all in their image," Hagga told him.

Bolts didn't look like any god that Kit had ever heard of. He stood eight feet, long-limbed, and rawboned. He had skin as white as snow, a hollow for a nose, a slit for a mouth, and huge black on black eyes the look of oil. Bolts wasn't really his name. His Al'tkash name was incomprehensible even after the nano had reprogrammed Kit's brain to understand alien speak, so he took to calling him Bolts for the fact that he had a bundle of bolts that were actually bones rising like a crown from the top of his head. It wasn't a very creative name, but Bolts didn't mind.

"You're here to fight, to compete, and to win." Bolts had told him on his very first day of training. "You were chosen to represent your world because you're young. Which means you're easy to train, less likely to resist, and less likely to reject the nano."

The nano were machines the size of atoms that lived in all things, across all the worlds of the Masters. They quickened reflexes, strengthened muscles, healed wounds, slowed aging, they killed men and even brought them back from death.

Hagga said that they were a gift from the gods bestowed on the Masters. Sacred duty entrusted to the clergy by the divine creators. The grinders told him that they were ancient tech, existing long before the Masters, built by some long dead civilization. The priests, in their opinion, were nothing more than grifters with engineering skills.

Whatever the truth, only the Masters knew how to control and manipulate the nano to their will, giving them the ability to bend time and space, even alter reality. Their Champions, immortal, incorruptible, mighty, could move as a flash, and slice whole armies to pieces. In ten thousand years no one had defeated them, few worlds tried to resist them, those that did had been wiped clean of life. This was why the Masters ruled the galaxy, and all other species served as their slaves.

Kit's dad had told him about slavery. How people used to own people and treat them like animals. Working them to the bone and punishing them brutally with whips and chains when they'd disobey or try to escape. Slaves were considered lesser, inferior, soulless. Kit didn't know if he had a soul or not but he didn't like the idea of being a slave, of his mom and dad being slaves, of his little brother being a slave, annoying though he could be.

"You have only one chance to save your world," Bolts told him, "win the game. Win the game and save your world."

Elimination combat by melee weapon. Forty-four fighters representing forty-four worlds, each trained in seclusion by a former fighter, each vying for one prize: ascension.

"Why me?" asked Kit.

"You're here, what does it matter?" was his trainer's reply.

But still the question nagged him. All he had was the training, the gym, and his cell. The milkwomen only came at mealtimes and the grinders only to tend to the equipment. And Bolts, Bolts rarely said a word to him. Only: "faster, human" and "slower, human" or "again, human."

So the question kept coming back, again, and again, until his head would hurt. As he learned to fight and dodge and leap and run, as he dreamt the same dream every night, as the day of the games grew nearer, Kit puzzled, obsessed, and theorized.

Maybe there is no reason? he thought. Maybe it's just dumb stupid luck.

So it went until one day when Kit stepped out into the gym to begin his routine – stretches, running, lifting, gravity training, dueling – that Bolts told him, "No more training. Today you rest and tomorrow we board a transport for the capital."

"Are we going to the games?" asked Kit.

"The games, yes," said Bolts, his face, his large black eyes, expressionless. His mouth a slit.

"Am I ready?" asked Kit.

"You are," was the other's simple reply.

***

It was hard for him to leave the gym. As he traded in his grey training uniform and helmet for a blue jumpsuit Kit found himself staring, saddened at his home for the last three years. When he first arrived at the age of ten he hated everything about the place. He'd spent countless hours in those first few weeks, at all hours of the night, scouring every nanometer of the gym, his cell, the mess, for some way to escape. Out of there, off world, to run home.

It was a hopeless fantasy. He was millions of light years from home. Even if he had managed to escape his rooms and the compound beyond them, even if he managed to find a ship and board it, how would he ever know how to fly it? How could he ever hope to find Earth?

Kit wasn't allowed to take anything save for his sword. It was a slightly curved, long sword with a silver, rubberized grip, simple silver guard, and a brilliant, shimmering, thin blue blade. "The Masters call it hypnotic steel," Bolts told him a year into his training. "From now on it is a part of your arm."

Hypnotic steel was lighter than air but stronger than anything found on Earth. Stronger than anything in the known universe if the grinders were to be believed. It could cut through wood, stone, flesh and bone cleanly in one strike. But it couldn't kill, at least not in Kit's hands. The nano were too quick. Instantly they'd repair the damage. Even an attempt at decapitation left little more than a bruise and a stiff neck. Through his years of training, Kit had been cut and stabbed thousands of times. At first the sensation was terrifying, but eventually one got used to the pain.

"Only the Masters are fast enough to kill with a blade," said Bolts.

It was said that to kill with a blade, even a hypnotic blade, a fighter had to be faster than light. It was the only way to do enough damage before the nano had time to repair it. The speed disrupted their cohesion, the grinders had said.

All the fighters in the games would use weapons forged with hypnotic steel. Some would use spears, others knives and daggers, fist weapons, great swords, axes, sickles, picks, and polearms. Bolts had trained him in them all, but first the sword. The sword was more elegant, he told him. "What you lack in brute force you'll make up for in agility."

He trained him hard. How to hold the sword, how to wield it, how to thrust, stab, slash, and block. Bolts worked his arms so hard he could barely lift them, and when he couldn't lift them they worked harder still.

"Your opponent won't care how tired you are," said his trainer.

At night, exhausted, Kit spent long hours gazing at the blade of his sword. It was called a hypnotic blade for the way it shimmered. *The nano again,* he thought. At first he daydreamed about being fast enough to kill Bolts, then the Masters, but would always feel guilty for it. He didn't want to kill anybody, he just wanted to go home.

As Kit slung his sword case onto his back he took another long look at the gym. After a few moments he realized that Bolts was staring at him from the door.

"A prison becomes a home after a time," said the trainer, then turned and left, his robe rippling as he stepped over the threshold.

Kit hadn't quite known what to expect beyond the door. He only retained scenes of his arrival. Unfamiliar planets and faraway stars. Pillars of light and colossal machines. No narrative. Just fragments.

Now Kit stepped out into a long empty corridor, a tunnel of glass and steel. Surrounded on all sides by a cold, dead, dark world, and a galaxy of strange and beautiful stars hanging above. As he walked to catch Bolts, his steps echoing off the metal plate, he noticed that the light of the stars caught and reflected against the formations outside the windows. They were ice crystals, millions of them, each larger than the last. It was like walking out amidst starlight, above and below, shining at them from every direction.

"Did you want to stay and stare?" asked Bolts.

"I didn't know it looked like this outside," said Kit.

"Here it does," agreed Bolts. "In other places it looks different. Matters not now. You'll never see this place again."

After a while the corridor met with others, each silent, empty, stretching for what looked like kilometers. Eventually the corridors merged into a large hallway. Above them, through the glass, Kit could see domes and towers rising, the shadow of more corridors and tunnels black against the heavens. The compound was massive, with enough space for what seemed like thousands, and yet there was only him and Bolts. *Are we the only ones here? Or are they hiding from us? From me?*

They followed the hallway for what seemed a long time until they came to a set of doors covered with the symbols of the Masters. Here a group of grinders worked at several computer terminals, chattering amongst themselves happily, falling silent only when trainer and fighter approached. One of the larger of the gang, who Kit thought he recognized, tapped his screen and the doors slid open with a heavy sigh.

On the other side gases exploded and machines worked furiously connecting and disconnecting hoses, raising and lowering platforms. As a gust of air hit them, Kit brushed a few strands of his dark hair away from his dark eyes, and only then realized that he was looking at a starship, sitting in a launch tube, pointing upward toward the sky.

Without a word Bolts started forward again, and as Kit began to follow he understood that they were really leaving for good. Then he thought about the milkwomen, about Hagga, and regretted not having had a chance to say goodbye.

As they approached the mammoth ship, curved, and bulbous, rising several hundred meters above them, they came to a gravity well much like the ones that Kit had trained on for the last three years. Kit didn't hesitate to step on the pad and was immediately hurled into the air, up along the ship's fuselage, twisted, spun, and deposited on a platform several dozen meters above the ground. Playing on the gravity wells was one of the few facets of his training that he enjoyed. He took to it like a fish to water, or so Bolts might say if his world had any fish. In the games, he knew, gravity wells were placed throughout the arena to make the fights more entertaining, to add an element of uncertainty.

"Knowing how to move in the arena is just as important as knowing how to swing a sword," Bolts had told him.

Off the platform was a round hatch that led into a long corridor and then to a cabin with several rows of pods staring up at them. They were sleep pods, designed to allow passengers to remain in stasis for the duration of prolonged space flight. The grinders had told him about sleep pods, and about space journeys that might last decades, but they had also told him about great planet-sized ships that the Masters had built that could tear holes in the very fabric of space and jump instantly from one corner of the galaxy to another.

Kit hesitated and looked back to Bolts who was coming up behind him down the corridor, slouched over as not to hit his head. The ship was clearly not designed for someone of his stature.

"How long is it to the capital?" he asked.

"The journey will take months," came the reply. "The capital is several light years away."

That was surprising. Kit had picked up enough to know that the training center wasn't on the same planet as the capital, but he thought for sure it was in the same system.

"We'll arrive before the games begin," explained Bolts, "in the meantime you'll sleep and learn, while I fly the ship."

"Learn?" asked Kit.

"Sleep pods are designed to interact with your implant and keep the mind active during flight, I've programmed several years of lessons into the computer. Combat, strategy, science, history." As though anticipating his next question, Bolts added, "Your mind will process information faster in stasis."

Kit nodded, looking down at the rows of pods. "Are there other passengers?"

"No other passengers," said Bolts.

Kit let out a breath he hadn't realized he was holding and lowered himself down into the cabin. After stowing his sword case in a nearby bin he laid himself down in the front most pod. Bolts came down next to him, strapped him in, and entered a few commands onto a touchscreen. Suddenly a glass sheet came down with a hiss and a snap, and within a heartbeat the lights flashed and dimmed, and all went to black.

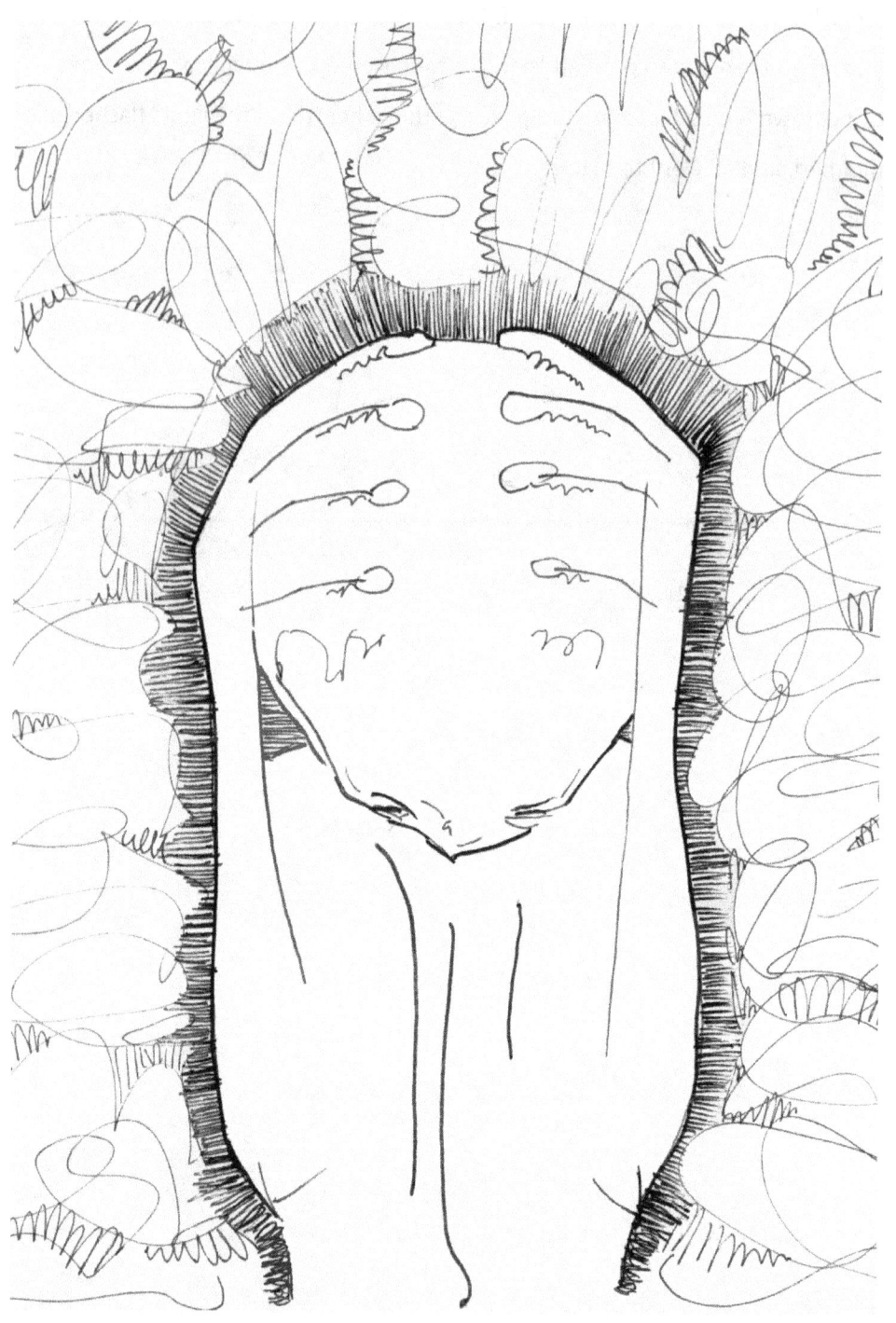

14 **kp dawes**

Chapter 2: Egg

Kit was sitting at a desk in a classroom surrounded by a group of students, from a dozen different worlds. He didn't recognize any of their kind save for one, a small Al'tkash boy, about his age, seated next to him. He looked like Bolts in miniature, bony features, big black eyes, and all. In front of them stood a human woman with short brown curled hair, wearing glasses, a flower print dress. She smiled.

"Good morning, Kit," she said happily. "It's wonderful you could join us today. My name is Ms. Moffat and I'll be your teacher for the duration of our journey."

"Hello, Ms. Moffat," said the class as one.

She smiled more broadly and said, "Before we get started, can anyone tell me the Three Pillars of Imperial Hegemony?"

A small bald boy in the second row, who looked very human except for his grey skin and striking violet eyes, raised his hand and said, "Duty, Unity, and Obedience."

"Very good, absolutely right," said Ms. Moffat. "And do you know who first said those words?"

"Epheus d'Aron, also known as Epheus the All Knowing," responded violet eyes. "The first Lord Emperor."

"Correct again!" said Ms. Moffat as the walls of the classroom dissolved replaced by stars and a large blue planet, surrounded by a network of orbital platforms and a pair of bright twin moons.

"Epheus," said Ms. Moffat, "great father, first god amongst mortals, first Master, nurturer of machines, unifier of tribes, conqueror of the stars."

"More like thief, murdered, and slaver," whispered the Al'tkash boy.

Kit snickered as Ms. Moffat continued. "This is Nos, first of the link worlds, the center of the known universe, capital of the Empire for the last ten thousand years and our final destination on this journey. It is home of the present imperial court, the great mother, and site of the centennial games." She glanced at Kit. "Can anyone tell me why Epheus began the games?"

Another child with long limbs, long neck and small head responded, "To find worthy citizens among the savage species."

Ms. Moffat clapped her hands excitedly and said, "Very, very, good. To find worthy species. Exactly right." The walls changed again to an aerial view of a glass domed coliseum in the heart of a city larger than any city on Earth. "The games, held every one hundred years, are an opportunity for lesser species like us to prove ourselves worthy of becoming citizens of the Empire. Winners and vanquished both. Already over four thousand worlds have been indoctrinated in this way, seventy-nine ascended to full citizenship in the Empire."

"But isn't there honor in servitude?" asked violet eyes.

"Of course there is," said Ms. Moffat firmly. "Of course there is. To serve the Masters in any capacity is to be awash in the light of the gods. The Masters eliminate disease, hunger, suffering, slow the process of aging, and in return all they ask is obedience. This is why it is not uncommon for fighters at the games to yield before the first battle. There is much honor in coming willingly to service."

"I hear the slaves that come willingly only get beat half as much," whispered the Al'tkash boy. Kit laughed out loud and was rewarded by a glare from Ms. Moffat.

"Are the Masters gods?" asked violet eyes.

Ms. Moffat said, "None but our Lord Emperors who are gods in the flesh."

"The Lord Emperors are gods then?"

"Upon leaving their mortal form they ascend to a higher realm, this is true."

"How many Lord Emperors have there been?" asked another student.

"Seven," said Ms. Moffat, the walls behind her shifting to reveal four men and three women. Masters. Tall, radiant, and beautiful, each with glimmering metallic, silver veins that made them appear almost ethereal. Kit knew enough about the Masters to know that their appearance was the result of tens of thousands of years of manipulation of the nano. Once they had been not at all different from humans, now they were as much machine as they were animal.

Ms. Moffat went through each of the seven, speaking of their accomplishments until she settled on the last, a man of strong aquiline features, slender but solidly built, his scalp hairless. He had a look darker than the rest. "And finally our great lord and protector for the last nine hundred years, Aejus'lobine, victor at the Battle of the Four Pillars, conqueror of the Highborne, builder of the World Ship."

"And killed more worlds than the other six combined," said the Al'tkash boy to Kit.

"Does the Lord Emperor come to the centennial games?" asked violet eyes.

"He has been present at the previous eight," responded Ms. Moffat, the walls shifting again, to a view of the arena from the game floor, the walls sloping up to stands, a great pavilion at their center. "He will of course be in attendance for this one as well."

This time it was Kit who raised his hand. "Do the Masters ever fight in the games?"

The other students started laughing until Ms. Moffat silenced them with her hand. "The Masters of course have their Champions, but no one could ever defeat them. No, the games are only for lesser species. A proving ground. A test of will and strength."

"But they can be challenged," said the Al'tkash boy loudly.

Ms. Moffat knit her brows and said, "Yes, a challenge can be made to fight a Champion, but it would do no good. Savages have no hope of defeating the Masters."

Kit and the Al'tkash boy exchanged a glance.

"All right class," said Ms. Moffat as the walls became walls again, "take out your screens and we'll read through The Articles of Bondage. I expect everyone to memorize *The Hymn of Thralldom* before we move on to Xenobiology and Beginner's Arena Tactics." She looked Kit in the eyes, "I'm expecting great things from you."

Kit pulled his screen from his desk, powered it up and found the appropriate lesson already displayed. As he let out a sigh and settled in to read the first line of The Articles of Bondage, a message popped up.

MY NAME'S EGG.

He glanced over to see the Al'tkash boy smiling at him. He shot him a smile back and typed:

HI, EGG. I'M KIT.

They exchanged another smile and Egg gestured toward Ms. Moffat, standing at the head of the class, watching the students go about their assignment.

DON'T BELIEVE HER. SHE LIES.

Kit leaned over his screen, moving his arm to make sure Ms. Moffat couldn't see what he was doing.

HOW DO YOU KNOW?

Egg hesitated a moment before responding.

DON'T MATTER, BUT I'LL TEACH YOU IF YOU WANT.

Kit looked at the other and gave him a nod.

"What are you doing?" asked Ms. Moffat suspiciously.

Kit cleared his screen at once and said, "Memorizing the *Hymn of Thralldom*, as assigned, Ma'am."

The Earth woman glared at him a moment but said nothing else.

So began Kit's education. During class time he'd listen to Ms. Moffat and play the role of the dutiful student, answering questions, completing assignments as was expected. After hours, after Ms. Moffat and the other students would vanish to wherever they came from, he'd get the real story from Egg, unedited and uncensored. Tales of slavery, misery, and genocide.

There was something familiar about Egg that Kit trusted inherently.

"Why even bother?" asked Kit one day. "Why even have the games? Why not just enslave everyone?"

"The Masters value strength above all else," responded Egg. "So they make worlds compete. Partly for entertainment and partly because they to think of themselves as generous to lesser species. They know that the best way to keep the link worlds docile is to throw them some scraps. Offer the appearance of upward mobility. One world is given citizenship and the task of controlling those that it vanquished."

"So if I win, Earth will have to help enslave the worlds that lose?"

"It's a great system."

As they went Egg taught Kit more than just history. He told him about gravity well strategies not covered in the official arena tactics manuals, styles of fighting not expressly allowed in the games rulebooks, ran countless hours of vids of past victors and losers, taught him the topography of the barracks where he'd be staying, of the capital cities, and even basic starship design and aviation.

"You never know when you might want to get off planet in a hurry," said Egg with a wink and a smile.

They used the walls of the classroom for their lessons, just as Ms. Moffat did for hers. And soon Kit realized that he could project his own thoughts, his own memories on those four walls.

It seemed like weeks went by this way. Maybe months.

More than anything else Kit loved having Egg's company. He hadn't played with another kid in years. It felt good to laugh, and hide, and have secrets again. It was strange to think that Egg and Bolts were of the same species. Whereas Egg was talkative and funny, Bolts never laughed, never even smiled, barely had said more than two sentences at a time in all the three years Kit had known him.

In between his lessons, there were always his dream. Earth. Michigan. Dad reading. Mom and brother doing crafts. Workmen outside, building. Rodney Richter and Chris Caputo laughing. When, after some months, he showed Egg his dreams up on the classroom walls the other said, "On my world dreams were sacred. We worshipped dreams. They led us places."

"What do you think it means?" asked Kit.

Egg shook his head, "Only the dreamer knows."

Four months in stasis seemed more like four years to Kit. Four years spent with Egg, during which neither of them aged or felt pain. Once, about halfway through, Kit had a vision that he was back in the sleeping pod, half awake. His father sitting next to him on the other side of the glass. Kit tried to lift his hand and reach his father, but his limbs wouldn't work and soon darkness took him. He didn't know what the vision meant, but Kit felt such profound sadness afterward that the next day in class he could barely concentrate on the lesson.

A person could live a whole lifetime in stasis, the grinders had told him. And from Egg he learned about whole civilizations that drifted through space for thousands of years asleep. Dreaming of lifetime upon lifetime, until after a while there was no way to tell dreaming from reality or reality from dreaming.

"Why do some species ascend while others do not?" asked Ms. Moffat one day, cheerfully.

"Ascended species are those that have won at the games," responded violet eyes.

"And what makes a winner?"

"Being the best and strongest," he responded.

"That's how they win, but what makes a winner?" asked Ms. Moffat.

The walls of the classroom faded and were replaced by video of combat in the coliseum. An alien with spotted skin and blood-red eyes, wielding a polearm was locked in battle against a massive, armored, tank of a creature with three sets of horns on its head, holding not one, but two great battle-axes.

"A Suul-Manee fighter was able to defeat a Boduk in under a minute," said Ms. Moffat, as the spotted fighter leapt over her massive opponent and buried her polearm in the other's chest. "How?"

There was a stir in the class.

"You recall our lesson on Boduk physiology? The Boduk was clearly stronger and faster," she continued. "So why did the Suul-Manee ascend and not the Boduk?"

Silence.

"In a word," said Ms. Moffat, "destiny. The gods blessed the Suul-Manee and rewarded them with ascension."

WHAT SHE MEANS IS THAT THE MASTERS ARRANGED IT.

"Why were they blessed above all others?" asked violet eyes as Kit keyed in a reply to Egg's message.

HOW DID THEY ARRANGE IT?

"Excellent question," said Ms. Moffat. "The gods direct all things. As they made *most* species in their image, they also direct the fate of species along specific paths. Those who prove themselves worthy over millennia are steered toward ascension. Those deemed unworthy into the bliss of eternal servitude."

THE TOURNAMENT IS FIXED.

"What makes a species worthy of ascension?" asked another student.

"In another word," replied Ms. Moffat. "Tenacity."

SO THE MASTERS HAVE A WINNER IN MIND?

"You must possess the determination to do whatever you can, whatever has to be done, no matter what," continued the teacher. "Only in this way can a species prove its exceptionalism."

NO. BUT THEY HAVE FAVORITES.

"What is *exceptionalism*?" asked violet eyes.

FAVORITES?

Ms. Moffat replied, "Exceptionalism is the belief that one is special above all others."

THE MASTERS DON'T CARE WHO WINS AS MUCH AS WHO LOSES. THEY DON'T WANT NON-HUMANOIDS AMONG THEIR RANKS.

"There are no rules?" asked Kit aloud.

Ms. Moffat met his eyes and said, "None beyond those of the Masters."

"So the Masters make up the rules as they go along?"

"Not exactly," said Ms. Moffat, carefully. "But what's a set of rules to the gods' chosen people?"

Later, after the others had cleared out, Kit turned to Egg and asked. "Isn't that a contradiction? How could someone be above the rules but still obey the Masters?"

Egg considered the question and said, "The Masters have no rules. They answer to no one and do whatever they want. But they expect all others to obey them. To ascend means to live the contradiction."

"Because ascended species aren't equals," said Kit.

"It's slavery in another form," responded Egg.

Kit turned away. Heat flashed across his face. In the months, years that he's spent in that classroom all he heard were lies. If losing was losing and winning was losing what was the point of any of it?

As though reading his mind, Egg got out of his seat and put a hand on his shoulder. "There are other ways," he said.

"What other ways?" asked Kit, feeling suddenly tired.

"Only the dreamer knows," replied Egg with a kind smile.

From then on something changed for Kit. In the following days and weeks it was harder for him to play along. Harder not to feel exhausted by the lie of it. More and more he wanted an end to it. To wake up and be done with Ms. Moffat, the other students, even Egg.

"Who can describe The Three Orders?" asked Ms. Moffat.

Violet eyes raised his hand and said, "Nobility, citizenry, and servantry. The nobility is the highest strata, made up entirely of Masters, and is divided between the royalty and aristocracy. The citizenry is generally not divided, but informally is made up of overseers and idlers. The servantry has several subclasses dependent on factors such as education and dominant biological traits."

"And the largest class is...?"

"The servantry," answered violet eyes immediately.

"Very good!" said Ms. Moffat happily, clapping.

Kit rolled his eyes and Egg snickered.

"Now," began Ms. Moffat with a sly smirk, the kind teachers get when they're about to ask a trick question. "Which class is the smallest?"

No one answered at first. The trap was there. As Ms. Moffat raised her brows expectedly, violet eyes blurted out, "The nobility?"

Ms. Moffat shook her head. "I'm afraid that's wrong."

Violet eyes lowered his head.

HE'LL NEVER BE THE SAME AGAIN.

Kit offered Egg a weak smirk as Ms. Moffat asked, "No one?"

"The priests," said Kit. "The priests are the smallest class."

Ms. Moffat beamed, "Very good, Kit!"

"But they're not really a class," he added quickly. "They don't really answer to anyone."

"That's a good point, Kit," said Ms. Moffat with a happy little nod. "The clergy is above the traditional social order. Although priests are selected from amongst the nobility, they answer only to the gods. Only the priests know the mysteries of the machines, first bestowed on Epheus at the dawn of creation."

Normally Kit would let it go there, unchallenged, unquestioned, as he had countless times before, as Egg always urged him to do, but today he felt different. For the first time in what seemed years he felt unbound by the constraints of the program.

"Why do only the priests know how the nano work?" he asked.

Ms. Moffat's smile waivered slightly, "Because it is divine will, of course. Epheus gave us the machines."

"Epheus was a god," said Kit.

"Exactly."

"But you taught us that Epheus was born mortal."

Ms. Moffat nodded, "Well remembered."

"But if he was a god wouldn't he always have been a god? How could a god be born mortal?"

"I don't quite know what you mean, Kit. Epheus was god and mortal both."

Kit considered and decided to change direction.

"So does even the Lord Emperor have to do what the priests tell him?"

Ms. Moffat's smile vanished. "That would never happen. Never. Among the Masters there is no disunity. They speak as one to fulfill the will of the gods."

"So there's never disagreement?"

"Never."

"Never?"

"Never."

"But what if the gods wanted one thing and the Lord Emperor wanted another?"

"Never."

"What if a Lord Emperor wanted to free all the slaves?"

"Don't use that word."

"Slaves?"

"It would never happen," responded Ms. Moffat, sternly. "It never could."

"But what if it did?" asked Kit, pushing. "Who would have the last word? The Lord Emperor or the priests?"

"All good comes from the Masters, generosity, forgiveness, love," she recited.

"Yes," said Kit, "but Masters could disagree, and if priests and nobles are both-"

"No, no, no!" Ms. Moffat huffed. "You are confusing things. It would never happen. Duty, Unity, and Obedience."

CAREFUL.

Kit ignored the message and asked, "What about civil war? Have the Masters ever gone to war against each other? On my world people used to fight each other all the time, even brothers against brothers."

"That's because you come from a savage world," she responded, turning red. "A savage, ugly world."

Kit ignored the attack. "Has a Master ever killed a Master?"

"What? What? No. That's enough!" she said.

"What if the gods told the Masters that slavery was wrong?"

"THAT'S ENOUGH!" she screamed.

"Slavery isn't love," said Kit.

"THAT'S ENOUGH!" she screamed.

"Slavery is evil!"

And abruptly the classroom was empty, no Ms. Moffat, no kids, no one, save for Kit and Egg.

"What happened?" asked Kit.

"You completed your lesson," responded Egg, getting out of his seat.

"Huh? What do you mean?" asked Kit as the walls shifted to reveal billions of stars. Except they weren't stars, they were galaxies, billions of galaxies, clusters, interwoven, brilliant stretching into forever.

Egg looked out over the cosmos and said, "Do you know why people believe in gods?"

Kit shook his head no.

"Hope," responded Egg. "Hope of salvation from the Masters."

"But the gods belong to the Masters," said Kit.

"The gods don't belong to anyone," said Egg.

Kit looked at him, then at the universe, turning slowly around them. "Was Epheus a god?"

"As close as a mortal can come to it," Egg responded. "And if there's one there can always be another." A smile crossed his small mouth.

"What happens now?" asked Kit.

"You fight. You win."

"And become like them?"

"You'll never be like them."

Kit wanted to tell him he was wrong. That human beings had done horrible things. But before he could respond Egg pulled him into his arms and embraced him tightly. It felt awkward at first. He couldn't remember the last time anyone touched him as not to hurt him. But after a moment he let himself relax and hugged Egg back.

"I always believed you," he said, his voice shaky.

"No," said Egg. "You listened. Today you started to believe. That was the whole point."

Kit shook his head. "I don't know what you want me to do," he said.

Egg didn't answer. He just held him, warmly. And they stayed like that for a long while, saying goodbye as the universe drifted around them. And much later, after he was unsealed from his sleep pod, after the grogginess of prolonged stasis finally began to wear off, as he sat wrapped in a blanket next to Bolts in the small flight cabin of their starship, the central planet of the Masters growing in the distance, Kit thought about Egg and all the people he'd never see again.

"I met a boy in there," he said quietly, staring off into the void of space through the cabin's window, as he felt the force of the thrusters push him back against his crash couch. "He was one of your people."

Bolts turned toward him as his fingers worked the ship's controls.

"But he wasn't like you," continued Kit, his brow furrowed. "He was happy. He talked to me."

Bolts turned back to his controls and after a few long beats of silence, and said, "I knew a boy like that once."

Kit looked at him, surprised. "You did?"

"I did," replied the other, eyes on the controls. "Not anymore. Not many of us left."

Kit brought his blanket tighter around himself. "Why not?"

Bolts punched a few numbers into the navigation computer, adjusting their course slightly. "After my games were done," he said, his voice even, "my people decided to resist the Masters rather than submit. It was a short war. Billions died."

Kit watched his trainer, his face unchanging, his concentration firmly on his task, and then turned back to the window. He thought about Egg's world, years, decades, perhaps centuries dead. He thought about all the dead worlds. He thought about Earth.

"Who was he?" he asked turning back to his teacher.

"Why would I know?" responded Bolts.

"You programmed it."

Bolts paused and said, "Probably just a ghost in the machine. I'll run a diagnostic. Purge the file."

"No," said Kit, "don't."

Bolts turned to him again, his large black, oily eyes studying him. "Why not?"

Kit shook his head, turning back to the window. "He was my friend."

Bolts stared at Kit for a second longer. A hint of a smile appeared and instantly disappeared at the edge of the trainer's small mouth, then he turned back to the ship's controls.

"As you wish," he said.

30 **kp dawes**

Chapter 3: Barracks

By the time Kit arrived at the barracks four fighters had already forfeited their worlds to the Masters. Each surrender was met with boisterous approval by the trillions of citizens who lived across the link worlds.

"There will be more," his trainer told him. "It's good. It means better odds."

Kit understood, but still it brought him no joy to hear. There was something wrong in it.

Bolts had docked their transport at one of the larger orbital platforms, floating above the sprawling central continent. From there they took a space elevator down to a processing station a few hundred kilometers from the capital. Then a maglev to the city itself. Despite the countless ships docking and leaving, the countless travelers coming to and from the planet, they passed through checkpoints quickly. Fighters weren't subject to the usual customs and contaminant screenings. They were important. Special.

In fact, Kit hadn't realized until they arrived that he was a celebrity of sorts. Not as much a celebrity as the nobility, or a vid star, but a famous curiosity all the same. Aliens would stare at him. Point at him. Make comments under their strange and exotic faces. They could tell that he was from someplace they'd never heard of, a species they'd never seen. In short, he was the alien here.

At every point, Kit was overwhelmed by the abundance of life. Its sights, its sounds, especially its smells, thick with musk and acidity. Hundreds of species lived and labored on the central planet and they cluttered every lift, walkway, and station at which they stopped. And at every opportunity they pressed against him. Touched him. Poked and prodded him.

Bolts did his best to keep them back, but there were too many of them. Always, everywhere, curious.

On the streets of the capital, where buildings of grass and stone and glass rose forever into the sky, dissected and bisected by roads, tram lines, walkways and terraces, there were animals too. Gargantuan beasts of burden, pets from every corner of the galaxy, wild things, strange things, beyond imagining. All things flow into the capital, it was said.

"How many of them are slaves?" asked Kit as they pushed their way through the crowded streets, dodging all manner of peddler, vendor, and huckster.

"Remember your lessons," responded Bolts, "only seventy-nine species have ascended."

In the Empire there was no need for collars, tattoos, brands, or papers. The difference between slavery and freedom was a matter of biology.

From what Kit could see Masters there were few. He knew from Egg that those who lived on Nos dwelled in the clouds, at the tops of the tallest towers, or on vast country plantations far beyond the noise and din of the cities. But even so, now and then, Kit would glimpse one of them. Lounging at the many crystalline pools, peering down from the ornate balconies that dotted every building, or carried in litters by slaves. They were even more magnificent than they'd been in the vids. Aglow in light, with eyes both mesmerizing and terrifying, silver veins shimmering against blue skin, the crowds parted like water before them.

For the first time Kit was confronted by the size of the Masters. Although thin and graceful, their scale was twice that of human beings. And like any creature possessing an overabundance of size and beauty, there was a perceptible cruelty about them.

"Welcome, fighter," said an emaciated creature, Kit knew as a Durg, from behind an array of displays at the entrance of the barracks. "World?"

"Earth," responded Kit, trying not to stare at the Durg's twisted, rail thin face.

"Kopper Io Talos," said the Durg in a steady shrill as he read off of one of the displays. "Human."

"Kit," said, Kit. "Only my mom ever called me Kopper."

The creature raised a flap of skin to reveal a bloodshot eye, looked Kit up and down, sighed loudly and went back to his work. "Are you planning to forfeit your world?"

Bolts glanced down at Kit, as he said, "No. Never."

The lack of hesitation seemed to take the Durg aback slightly, but he did not comment. He tapped a few entries into his screens and as a door slid open behind him, said, "You're room is ready. Welcome to the barracks, and may the gods be with you."

The barracks was a cavernous open building, with three levels of dormitories built in dark woods and grey stone around a full size practice arena, complete with mobile platforms and gravity wells. Above was a vaulted glass roof beyond which could be seen the dome of the coliseum, which was connected to the barracks by way of the Hall of Champions.

Kit stepped out to the railing and noticed about twenty others fighters, representing various worlds, standing or sitting along the railing across all three levels of the dormitory. All eyes were down to the practice arena where two fighters were in the midst of combat.

One was short, squat, and heavy, with a thick, fat brow and wild brown hair under his helmet. In the right light he might have maybe passed for a stout human boy, but for the two extra arms growing out of his sides. In each he had a dagger, short and sharp, and glowing of hypnotic steel. The other was slender, tall, and muscular, with elongated limbs. He looked almost a decade older and stronger than his opponent, with burnt hair, fierce dark, lined eyes, and tattoos all over, showing across the exposed arms and chest of his custom cut battle suit. He was armed with a long spear, with hypnotic blades attached at either end.

Kit wasn't sure why he was having a hard time focusing on the tall boy until he noticed that he seemed to blur as he ran. And then he realized that the boy's tattoos weren't tattoos at all but some kind of pigment that played havoc on the eyes.

Kit guessed that the effect must have even been more dizzying up close, because every time the round, wild boy tried to lunge at the other he lost his balance slightly, knocking him off stride. The tall boy seemed to enjoy his opponent's confusion, because every time he had an opportunity to strike true he'd veer off and circle, sometimes jabbing him with the point of his spear, just enough to cause pain, but not enough for the computer to register a win.

"Why are they fighting each other now?" asked Kit. "Aren't they afraid they'll reveal their strengths?"

"Not as much as they hope to expose their opponents' weaknesses," responded Bolts.

"It's stupid," said Kit.

Bolts shrugged. "Much can happen in the barracks that can change the equation in the games."

The wild boy, grown frustrated by his opponent's abuse, shouted something that Kit couldn't make out and suddenly jumped onto a gravity well.

Instantly he was flung sideways around the arena. In the same instant the tall boy used his spear to vault himself onto a moving platform and at an unexpected speed bounded from platform to platform, jumping across them like a frog would across a river.

By the time the wild boy landed at the far end of the arena the tall boy was already on him, spear in hand. He was a blur of brutality. The wild boy managed to block one, two, three strikes, but within moments had lost two daggers and was fumbling not to lose a third.

The tall boy went for a jab to the other's stomach, but somehow the wild boy managed to dodge and grab onto a moving platform with two of his four hands. The tall boy didn't lose a beat. He half ran up the sloping arena wall and pushed himself off landing onto the same platform just as the wild boy gained his balance.

The wild boy attacked with his two remaining daggers, trying to use his mass to his advantage, hoping to drive his opponent off the platform, but it was no good, the tall boy was faster and his attack too disorienting. Three more hits and the wild boy was down to his last remaining dagger, staggering with each slice. As the wild boy faltered the tall boy planted his spear again and used it to spin in a half circle, knocking the other off the platform and onto his back. The wild boy tried to throw one of his daggers, but it was too late, moving deftly the tall boy leapt into the air once more, shifted his spear and drove the blade deeply into his opponent's chest. The wild boy let out a whimper, as the other twisted the spear, before finally removing it bloody and wet.

"Winner, Tau Abravin Morsh, Ifis," announced an automated voice over the speakers. "Combat time: 6 minutes, 14 seconds."

Kit felt sick to his stomach as he watched the winner, Tau make his way off the arena floor, spear in hand, a swagger in his walk.

"He enjoyed beating him," said Kit as he switched his focus to the wild boy struggle to his feet, dazed, rubbing at the point where he'd been stabbed, the wound already mended by the nano in his veins.

Bolts regarded him for a moment and said, "Use it against him."

"How?"

"Confidence can be weakness," was the other's reply.

Kit's room was nothing to write home about. Up on the third tier, not far from the doors leading to the Hall of Champions, it had a bed, lamp, four lockers with an adjoining washroom. Small and spartan, but built out of the same dark woods as the rest of the barracks, it felt much warmer than his metallic cell back at the training facility. Two of the lockers were empty, one to stow his jumpsuit, another to stow his sword between practice rounds and combat. The others contained a fitted battle suit, black with charcoal trim, and a hypnotic steel helmet with a retractable glass faceplate. Kit removed the battle suit. Embroidered on the breast was *Kit*, embroidered on the right shoulder was *Earth*, below that was a round patch, white on black, a circle at the center, lines radiating outward.

"What's this?" asked Kit.

"It was a symbol of my people before the Masters came," said Bolts from the doorway.

"For luck?"

"As you say," the other responded.

Kit closed the locker and asked, "What now?"

"Exercise and training in the mornings. The computer will tell you where," said Bolts, gesturing to a wall screen. "Afternoons are yours. Rest. Meditate. Once the games begins, combat will be in the evenings."

"When will the games begin?"

"Days," said Bolts, unflinching.

Kit nodded, and with a glance around the room, asked, "Where will you be?"

"Trainers' dorm, a building adjoining this one."

"Will you be with me for the fights?"

"Always," was his reply.

"I–" Kit wasn't sure what he was feeling or what he wanted to say, so he settled on, "Thank you."

"You are ready," said Bolts.

Kit nodded. "I know."

After his trainer departed, Kit stripped off his jumpsuit and got under the shower. He cranked it up hot, to let the water scorch off his journey and smiled at the realization that he hadn't technically washed in over four months. *Dad would kill me*, he thought.

Kit's smile faded. He slid down to the shower floor, bringing his legs to his chest. And for a while he watched the water fall and drain away, fall and drain away. He'd trained hard. He'd learned much. But he'd also forgotten. Forgotten what it was like to be a kid. Forgotten what it was like to have a family. Forgotten what it was like to feel safe. But they weren't safe, none of them, and they were counting on him to save them, whether they knew it or not.

But what if I don't want to save them? he thought, and all at once he hated himself for thinking it.

The water was burning hot, at first it had felt good against his skin, but now it only seemed to numb him, inside and out. He brought his hand up to the side of his head, and mindlessly ran a finger over the edge of the small metallic implant protruding from the skin beneath his hair. Then he watched the water. Fall and drain away. Fall and drain away.

38 **kp dawes**

Chapter 4: Ash

Kit awoke with a start and realized he was starving. By the display on the wall screen he could see it was dinnertime. He had slept through lunch and most of the afternoon and it took him a full minute to realize it was still the same day. Four months of sleep and he was still tired.

He got up out of bed, slid into his jumpsuit, evened his dark hair with his hands and walked out the door. The lights were already on throughout the barracks, a rich, yellow glow emanating from beneath the columns and along the edge of the walls. The practice arena was lit up too, bright and vivid, though empty at the moment. Kit made a note to practice in the same conditions. Combat would take place in the evenings, under the same kind of artificial light. As he made his way toward where he assumed he'd find the mess, he glanced up to the glass ceiling, where the setting sun had bathed the tall silver and green towers, and the dome of the coliseum, in a burning orange light.

The orientation of the barracks was not entirely dissimilar to that of the training facility that had been his home for three years, except scaled up considerably. To the north were the golden doors to the Hall of Champions, a long corridor leading to the coliseum floor. To the east were the training rooms and fight simulators, and beyond that the doors leading to the trainers' dorm. To the south was the barracks' entrance. And to the west the mess hall, and overseer's office.

As Kit walked into the mess he immediately felt eyes on him. There were no trainers here, no adults, they were all in their own dorm, here there were only fighters, most of whom had already been at the barracks for days, maybe weeks. Cliques had formed already. Small groups gathered at tables whispering and staring as Kit walked past, heading toward the food processors at the far end of the room.

Thanks to Egg's lessons Kit immediately recognized most of the species that he saw. There were a handful of insectoids and reptilians from the fringe systems spread across two tables. All were bipedal and much smaller than Kit had expected. They would be weaker than him, he knew, but faster and more agile. The one exception being an armored spider from a planet called Mrith, who, according to gossip, was the most ferocious and dangerous among them.

In a corner, all by himself, sat a wall of a creature, nearly five meters tall, all armor from head to foot that called itself a Soof but who everyone else called a rocknid. Long reach and blows that could bludgeon a fighter instantly, but slow of thought and ignorant on strategy.

In another corner sat a large hairy creature that looked a lot like a lean, upright grizzly bear with an ugly jaw and sharp claws that Egg had called an Optwap. Fast, strong, and furious, preferring its claws to melee weapons. Not far from him sat a tall, slender, and skinless lifeform that Egg called a Tobrus from the planet Tobra.

The rest of the beings were creatures much like Kit, sitting in twos and threes, grouped usually by physical similarities or common cosmic address.

Tau, the tall boy who had crushed his opponent with a double bladed spear, commanded the largest faction. A group of eleven boys, Kit assumed them all to be boys, sitting at a table in the middle of the mess.

All looked to be from what Egg had called the crafted worlds. Systems from a cluster closest to the link worlds, who were believed to have originated as the result of ancient genetic manipulations by a long dead species known only as the Makers. Sixty-five of the seventy-nine species ascended to citizenship originated from the crafted worlds. All had similarly tall and slender body structures, with elongated limbs, smooth, muscular, nearly translucent skin, and facial characteristics not unlike those of humans, varying mainly only in color and other seemingly cosmetic features.

Kit instantly recognized two blue B'tids from the twin worlds iB and iD. A yellow-skinned Ustion from Ustia. And a bleary-eyed, Ystrofaun from a rock called Ukfaun that was only a decade from complete ecological collapse. As Kit passed their table, Tau whispered something to his clique that sent ripples of laughter echoing throughout the room.

Still and silent, Kit reminded himself as he got to the end of the room. *The moment your enemy unnerves you he wins.*

Kit swiped a command on the food processor screen, identifying himself as human and as he waited for his tray heard the unmistakable sound of a chair hitting the floor. A moment later came a voice from behind him, "Hey, monkey boy, did anyone ever tell you that you smell awful?"

Do other worlds have monkeys? Kit thought as he straightened his back and glanced over his shoulder. One of Tau's minions, plum colored skin, ridges on his nose and forehead, orange eyes the look of glass marbles, was standing about a dozen paces behind him, hands clenched into fists. From what Kit remembered his people called themselves Bluecards and their world World, and had very literal, although often confusing names for everything.

"Did you hear me monkey boy?" said the Bluecard loudly, performing for the room and for his gang who were laughing uproariously at their table. "I said you smell like boasum butt!"

Maybe a boasum is like a monkey? Kit thought, keeping his eye on the boy but otherwise standing absolutely still. He didn't have his sword on him, and even if he had, weapon use was prohibited outside of training and combat. Hand-to-hand was hopeless, the boy easily had fifty pounds on him and was most likely faster besides. He had to improvise. And he had to be effective. If he lost now he'd have to fight them around the clock, in the coliseum and in the barracks.

"Are you deaf, monkey boy?" bellowed Bluecard. "Or are they mute as well as ugly on your world?"

Just then the food processor dinged and Kit's tray slid out. On it was a bowl of protein meal, an assortment of biologically compatible fruits and vegetables, and a bottle of water.

"Guess you're as big of a coward as you smell!" shouted the boy behind him.

Kit picked up his bowl of protein meal, scooped up a bite with a spoon and tasted it. Bland but hot. He put it aside on the counter and picked up the plate of fruits and vegetables. He didn't recognize any of them, couldn't even guess which corner of the galaxy they might hail from, but that was not unusual. He gave them a sniff and placed the plate next to his bowl. Finally he grabbed the water and took a good long swig. It was sweeter than what he was used to.

"Stop playing with him," shouted Tau from his table. "Teach the monkey boy some manners!"

They all laughed again, Bluecard most of all.

In that instant, Kit seized his empty tray, turned, and threw it with his full strength. The Bluecard hadn't expected it, and the tray smashed him in the face, slicing across his nose, black red blood gushing. He grabbed at his face, the nano in his system already repairing the gash, he roared with anger and might have charged if not for the fact that Kit had already closed the distance between them.

Kit kicked him in the groin, thankful that most aliens had the same basic biology, and swept his legs from under him. Then he was on him, hitting him, right, left, right, left. New gashes opened and closed, opened and closed, and the boy lurched with every hit. Kit knew that although the wounds would vanish, the boy felt every single punch, and he would feel them on for days.

It lasted seconds but it felt longer somehow. *Adrenaline probably*, Kit thought. And it wasn't until the only sound in the mess hall was the sound of fists pounding skin that he finally stopped.

Kit looked around. Everyone was staring at him, except for Bluecard, the boy with the plum skin, who lay unmoving on the floor, streaks of black red blood on his face.

Silently, Kit stood, retrieved his tray from the floor, walked back to the food processor, and placed his bowl of protein meal, his plate of fruits and vegetables, and bottle of water on top of it. Then he walked deliberately to a nearby table occupied by the wild boy with four arms who Tau had defeated that morning in the practice arena. As he put the tray down and slid into a seat, he noticed the wild boy gaping at him, eyes wide, mouth open, two forks, two spoons, clutched firmly in his mitts, unmoving.

"Hi," said Kit.

A couple of morsels of food that resembled carrot, dribbled out of the boy's open mouth, and after staring at Kit for a good, long minute, he slowly slid out of his chair, tray, utensils, and cup in hands, and quickly scurried over to another table.

Oh well, thought Kit, as the other fighters cautiously went back to their dinner and hushed conversations. He'd be the topic of discussion tonight.

Out of the corner of his eye he could see a couple of Tau's boys help Bluecard to his feet, the boy looked disoriented, but otherwise alright.

Kit reached out for his bottle of water and suddenly noticed that his hand, peppered with the boy's blood, was trembling. Was it the adrenalin wearing off or something else? He wiped his hand on the leg of his jumpsuit and steadied himself.

He felt numb. Shouldn't he feel something? Remorse? He hadn't wanted to do it. He had only wanted to eat his dinner. It was the other boy's fault. It nagged him that he felt nothing.

Kit picked up his spoon and poked at his protein meal. He wasn't hungry anymore, but he also realized he couldn't just get up and leave either, that might be interpreted as a sign of weakness. He had no choice but to stay in his seat, picking at his food.

"It's true what they say about humans," came a voice, "you really are vicious."

Kit glanced up from his bowl to see a girl who looked a lot like a girl except for her grey skin, striking violet eyes, and line of tattooed glyphs etched on the side of her bald head. She stood over him, her tray in her hands, looking expectedly.

"Not very talkative are you?" she said before he could formulate a response, as she plopped her tray down and sat across from him. "You have the Al'tkash trainer. I hear he's not very talkative either, but one of the best in the universe." She leaned in and whispered, "Did you know that the Al'tkash Rebellion is why Lord Emperor Aejus'lobine built the World Ship?" She nodded knowingly as she sat back in her chair, regarded Kit for a moment and suddenly stuck out her hand so quickly that it made him jump. "My name's Ashvani Khergostraponi, but everyone just calls me Ash," she said.

He took her hand, shook it firmly. "Kit," he said, a small squeak in his voice.

She smirked at him, "So you do speak. Good throw with the tray, I was impressed, my gear set includes throwing knives so I should know. The rest was unexpected too, which was also good. It's true what I heard about your kind."

"I had no choice," said Kit, "if I didn't-"

"Then they would have come after you again and again," she said, cutting him off. "I know. The crafted worlds are closer so they've all been here for over a month, bored, harassing all the new arrivals. So, well done, just perhaps excessive. But as I said, I heard about your kind." She said rapidly, each word practically strangling the one before it. "Humans have a reputation. Killers and warmongers they say. Is it true you regularly war against one another on your world? Use mass destruction weapons on your own kind? I never knew what genocide was until I heard of the Masters," she paused, "and you."

Kit frowned. She was right that people fought wars, killed and died, but humans weren't as bad as the Masters. Were they?

"My trainer told me that there's a lot of excitement among the nobility about human ascension," she continued on, in her rapid-fire manner. "But also concern. You're stubborn they say. Problematic. And physically weaker than a lot of the other species here."

"Your biggest advantage will be your ferocity," Bolts had told him long ago. "It's a trait few other worlds possess. If we can hone that skill, your competitors will never see you coming."

"I don't want to be ferocious," Kit had told him.

"Then you'll lose," was his trainer's curt reply.

"My trainer was a servant in one of the great houses for decades after her defeat," continued Ash, barely stopping for breath. "She still hears things. But just because there's talk of you don't think that you'll win," she flashed a grin. "I plan to be the victor. And if I fight you I will crush you. You fight with a sword don't you? Actually I know you do. My knives make short work of swords.

You'll see." She poked something that looked like meatloaf with a fork. "I like you, you're easy to talk to. Though I know I probably shouldn't be talking to you. You know I expected you to be taller somehow. Are they all the same height as you on your world?"

The sudden silence made Kit realize he had food in his mouth. He swallowed, took a drink of water and said, "I'm still a kid."

"Of course you are," she responded quickly. "So is everyone here, though the craftees sure look way older and you can never tell with the insectoid or the reptilian species. And if that rocknid in the corner is a kid I'd hate to see what the grownups look like. Can you imagine? They must be as big as houses. And by that I mean big. I don't know the relative size houses on your world. On my world average grown height is about 1.7 meters, give or take. Obviously I'm not there yet, but I have no reason to assume I won't get there. From what I can see most species tend to fall around that same average, with the big exception of the Masters of course and a handful of others. The craftees seem taller, I know, on account of their elongated limbs, but from what I've studied they max out at 2 meters. Surprising when you consider it. I think that the Makers are responsible for most of the life in the galaxy, far beyond the crafted worlds. How else do you explain the relative narrowness of biological diversity across the entire galaxy? For instance, do you know the odds against just two species inhabiting the same galaxy with features as similar as ours? What about hundreds? Or thousands? Makes you stop and think doesn't it?"

Kit, stopped to think and said, "You talk real fast."

Ash scowled, then relaxed, then smiled, all in the blink of an eye, and said, "Yes, I do. I know. Cultural trait more than a genetic one. I'm from the lowlands, near the equator of my planet, a series of urban centers in what my people call the Great Basin. We all talk like this there. In the north and south things are different. Slower. I'm sorry."

"No, I like it," said Kit, sincerely. "I haven't really heard anyone talk so much in a long time."

Ash flushed, and said, "Back home, before all this, I was studying to be a genomist. Whereas other species look outward we look inward to get at the genetic past. All that a people were, all one's ancestors were, is stored in one's genetic material. To know one's ancestors, their wisdom, experiences, dreams, and thoughts, one needs only unlock the correct genetic data. This is why the loss of any one genetic line is a loss for all. My mothers were both genomists, as their mothers before them." She paused for a moment, "I suppose all that will change after the games. I miss my mothers, do you miss your mothers?"

"I only have one mother," said Kit. "I have a father too, and a brother."

"Yes," she said with a shake of her head. "Apologies, of course you do. I did know that."

"What do those mean?" asked Kit, pointing to her tattoo.

She brought her fingers to the glyphs imprinted on the side of her head, and said, "I'm sorry, I can't tell you. It's private. It's something for my people to know, not aliens. My intention is not to be rude. I will understand if you're offended."

"No," said Kit with a chuckle, "you don't have to tell me, it's alright."

Ash smiled at him warmly, then just as quickly frowned, placed her fork on her tray and said, "When this is over, one of us will be the victor, and an overseer, and the rest will be slaves."

"I know," said Kit.

"I'm sorry, but I have to win," she said firmly. "I hope that does not affect our friendship."

Kit looked at her, at her hands folded behind her tray, at her serious demeanor and suddenly couldn't contain the laughter. Ash blinked at him, and within seconds was laughing along with him. They laughed so long and so hard that his cheeks hurt afterward and he had to take a gulp of water just to contain himself.

"See? Another universal trait," she said smiling. "Laughter, sadness, anger, pain in all of nature across the entire galaxy. Why? Why DNA? Why carbon? Yes, of course some species are more intense in certain areas, have some traits more pronounced, but that it should all develop so closely. It's amazing."

"Amazing," Kit agreed. "What did you do for fun back on your home world?"

Ash considered the question, biting at her lip, and responded, "My favorite thing to do was to sneak out of my morning classes early and go watch the suns rise over the Great Sea. There are these rock formations that jut out of the water, we call them the Matriarchs. And when the suns comes up behind them they look like they're dancing. I'd spend an hour each day just sitting by that water, thinking, writing, calculating ancestral lineages." She shook off the memory and asked, "What about you?"

He looked down at his cold protein for a moment, recalling the walks he took with his mom, the talks he had with his dad, the games he played with his brother. Finally he said, "There's this small town called Frankenmuth, a couple hours drive from our house. My parents used to take us there whenever they weren't working. In the summers they'd buy us taffy and let us ride on the ferry. In the winter they'd take us to buy ornaments and watch the Christmas lights." He paused for a moment, "I really liked those trips. Everyone was happy."

Ash raised her brows and said, "I didn't understand much what you just said."

They both laughed again. Even harder this time.

When they were done, Kit glanced around the mess and realized they were the only ones left. "I think we drove the others off," he said.

"Maybe we can use the same strategy to win," she offered with a grin.

"What do you want to do now?" he asked.

She considered the question for a moment, and then with a smirk, said, "Let's fight. Time to see if everything I was told about your kind is true."

Kit had decided that morning that he wouldn't practice outside of combat, that it was better to observe and that if anyone challenged him he'd forfeit, but somehow he found it hard to refuse Ash, so without much hesitation he agreed.

He went into his room and dressed in his black battle suit and shining hypnotic steel helmet. But as he took his sword in his hand he could hear Bolts in the back of his head, saying, "When you step into the arena you give everything you have or don't bother fighting at all."

By the time Kit got to the practice arena, the city beyond the glass ceiling of the barracks was lit up, the sky above black with night, except for the twin moons, one full, one not. Ash was already there waiting for him, wearing a battle suit like his except white, with two rows of knives set in pockets along her midsection in addition to the two she already had in her hands.

Blessedly, there were no eyes on them. The other fighters were most likely already in their rooms for the night or perhaps in the exercise room, working with their trainers.

"You ready?" asked Ash, as she lowered the visor over her face, the hypnotic steel helmet with shield being the one piece of equipment that would stop hypnotic steel from passing through, the only way to avoid a brain scramble.

Kit nodded to her and lowered his visor as well, then they proceeded to their respective far ends of the arena floor. Immediately as they stepped on to their start pads, the lights came on stronger, bathing them in blinding white light that made everything but the arena invisible, and the computer began the countdown from ten.

Ash had the advantage out of starting position, Kit knew. In the few seconds it would take him to close the distance between them, she could get two, three, even four shots at him with her throwing knives. He had to deflect and dodge, while still gaining ground, which would have the unavoidable side effect of making him an easier target.

...8, 7, 6...

Kit gripped his sword tightly in both hands, noting quickly the pattern of the moving platforms around and above him, along with the position of the gravity wells, variables that were automatically randomized by the computer for every match.

...5, 4, 3...

Still and silent. Kit could feel his breathing slow, training overtaking his reason center, countermanding his fear and flight response. He'd fought Bolts tens of thousands of times, had logged twice that many hours in fight simulators, but this was his first real test, practice or not. His first real opponent. Desperate, determined, the same burden on her shoulders that he felt on his own.

..2, 1, FIGHT!

As he moved off the start pad everything seemed to be happening slightly slower than was normal, like watching the action on a television moving at three quarters speed. But his mind was sharp, sharp as a razor. Sounds more acute. Smells more pungent. Colors more vivid.

Just as he had expected Ash let loose one knife and almost immediately after another. Kit dodged the first and deflected the second with his blade, but decided not to charge at her. Too much time. Too much exposure. In one fluid motion he leapt off to his side, onto a moving platform and from there onto another, deflecting a third blade as he rolled back to the floor and onto a gravity well. Using one of the tactics he'd picked up from Egg, he jumped and twisted himself as the force grabbed hold of him and shot him across the combat floor, increasing his speed considerably. He landed into a crouch about ten meters from Ash and just barely managed to avoid another knife, the blade clinking off the floor with a spark.

He smirked. Wasting no time, Kit grabbed hold of another platform that was speeding past, just as Ash vaulted backward making for another gravity well hoping to keep him at a distance. Rather than chase her, he moved to his side, and as she hit a gravity well, bound toward the north end of the arena, following the sloped wall, he hit his own and was hurled up and over in an elegant arc that came down on top of her.

They met with a clash of hypnotic steel, his sword against her knives, slash, counter, thrust, counter, block. Even at close range she sent two knives flying at him, so quickly that one slashed his shoulder, leaving a tear in his suit. But still, despite her fury, for Kit the fight unwound slowly, purposefully, every strike deliberate, every parry fluid and sure. He couldn't move any faster, but he had time to examine each movement, to study each blow.

He forced her back against the wall, she was down to her last two knives but as he moved to strike, she suddenly turned, ran into the wall, and jumped clear over his head. He turned with her and struck at her chest, but she dodged and thrust a quick blade at his leg. He felt the edge of it, not deep enough to end the fight, but sharp enough to make him wince.

From there the fight was point-to-point, fast and close and chaotic, he was backed up with no room, using his sword to keep her at a distance, but still she came. Again and again, her blades sparkling in the light of the arena. Up, down, always attacking.

And then suddenly he became acutely aware that she was slowing. Her movements were becoming more labored, her arcs wider, openings in her defense where none had been before. The change was so sudden that Kit had to restrain the urge to lunge, it smelled too much of a lure. She wanted him to go in, he realized. To get him close.

He smirked again, and feinted an attack, she closed in immediately, her knives swinging down at him hard, but he saw it coming and pulled back just as she was about to connect. Surprised, she raised her head, and swung again, but he had the advantage and swung hard against her. She lost one of her knives and lashed out hard with the other. He slid sideways and countered, hitting her fast and hard. Moving her back, keeping her shuffling.

She managed to dodge, rolled and slid, going for one of the knives she had thrown at him, laying on the floor a couple of meters away. He saw that too, and moved to intercept. Another clash, another thrust, another counter, and then everything froze as his blade came to rest against her neck, stopping just short of contact.

He opened his visor, "You're fast," he said, composed.

"I am," she agreed, then suddenly jumped and kicked, knocked his sword away, crouched and swept his feet from under him.

Kit collapsed hard onto his back and found Ash on top of his chest before he could even react, her blade at his neck.

He smiled. "Guess you win," he said.

"It's not a win until I deliver a killing blow," she said.

"So why are you hesitating?" he said looking up at her, squinting for the bright lights above her.

"Why did you?"

"We could always just leave the arena," he suggested.

"Then neither of us would win," she said. "Leaving the arena means forfeit."

"So let's forfeit," he said.

She frowned at him and slid down to sit next to him, replaced her last knife in a pocket, and said: "You're not what I expected human."

Kit raised himself on his elbows, "Bolts says that I should always do the unexpected."

"Bolts?" she asked.

"My trainer," he replied.

"Ah," she said, still catching her breath. "Your attacks were fast and hard. Harder than I thought."

And I'm not even tired, he thought. Ash hadn't pulled back, he realized, and even so she was a better fighter than anything he'd ever seen in a fight simulator. But somehow this fight felt different. Kit had felt different. More in control somehow.

"Thanks, Ash," was all he said. "You weren't so bad yourself."

She smiled at that. "I'll be better suited for our next encounter."

"So will I," he said returning her smile, still thinking.

After, they sat under the bright lights of the practice arena long into the night, talking about their families, and their home worlds, and their impressions of the capital. Now and again one of the other fighters would happen by, on their way from the exercise rooms or the simulators, maybe on their way to the mess for a late snack. They'd stare at the two of them for a minute, dressed in full battle gear, sitting under the moving platforms, weapons scattered about the floor, chatting happily. It was a strange sight to be sure.

When they finally decided to retire for the night, after retrieving their weapons, they stepped out of the arena together, the computer announcing a default match, by dual forfeit. "Combat time: 2 hours, 22 minutes, 56 seconds."

Chapter 5: Tau

Pholt was the barracks overseer and he wasn't at all happy with Kit.

"Unauthorized combat in the mess hall, improper use of a food tray, excessive use of the practice arena," he sighed heavily to the point where his whole body shuddered as he read the screen on his desk.

Phlot was a Mog. The Mog were one of the fourteen non-crafted ascended species in the Empire. Big and bulky, he looked like a hairless human man, except swollen up three times larger and as solid as oak. He spoke in a sort of monotone drone, which Kit thought had less to do with biology and much more to do with attitude. Phlot didn't seem to like his job.

"Well?" he asked unhappily, turning from his screen to Kit. "Do you have anything to say for yourself?"

Kit didn't really have anything to say for himself, but knew something on the order of acquiescence was required. So he said, "I'm really sorry. It will never happen again."

Phlot regarded him dispassionately for a moment. However lackadaisical the overseer might appear, Kit knew from Egg that the Mog were a brutal species. They were strong and unrelenting and in the five thousand years since their ascension had exterminated countless worlds. The Masters especially liked to send Mog troops in on the first waves of an attack, partly to hone Mog fighting skills, and partly to teach the Mog humility. Unlike the Masters the Mog were not invincible. Many millions had died serving the Empire. Many million more would die in the years and decades to come.

Phlot sighed heavily a second time and plucked something that looked like a tiny chocolate cube from out of a bowl on his desk and plopped it into his large uneven mouth. He chewed loudly for a moment, swallowed, and then said, "There's one like you ever century." His voice was even but still managed to somehow convey absolute annoyance. "Always from some galactic backwater of a world, who thinks that they can just do whatever they want. With no regard for rules and regulations. No respect for the authority of the Masters. But they all learn soon enough. When they lose their matches, when they fall off the roll, when their worlds are taken. They learn." He pointed a gigantic finger at him. "Just because you're a fighter and not yet technically a servant does not give you the right to do whatever you want. We have rules and regulations. You are obligated to follow those rules and regulations. Do you understand?"

Kit nodded. He wanted to tell him that the other boy started the fight, that no one else wanted to use the arena while he and Ash were talking, but he knew such protestations we're useless. Instead he said simply, "Yes, sir."

Phlot frowned at him and leaned back in his massive chair. "You know I'm a veteran. Fought a thousand campaigns. In hundreds of wars. I fought the Vosh, the Highborne, the Al'tkash. I was decorated. By the Lord Admiral of the Second Fleet himself," he waved a massive hand at a shelf full of awards and medals behind him. Each was polished, each was meticulously cleaned. "I was promoted to this post. I was asked for personally. A position of high honor." He shook his head. "And you know what? After all that I'm just a glorified babysitter. Wasting my time on this nonsense. On you." He tapped his screen and said, "the next time you get the urge to bash someone's face in do it in the arena in a battle suit. And for the love of the gods don't stop to have a conversation afterwards."

Kit nodded and stood to leave.

"And one more thing," said Phlot as he plucked another chocolate cube from the bowl, "don't think a flogging will hurt any less just cause those little robots in your bones sow you up between lashes. Ask your trainer if you don't believe me. Discipline is a way of life in the Empire. Discipline and duty."

As Kit left the overseer's office he found Ash waiting for him outside. "Did you get in trouble?" she asked.

"I got off with a warning," replied Kit as they started heading toward the training rooms on the other end of the barracks.

"Well that's good," said Ash with some relief. "What happened in the mess hall was self-defense pure and simple. There were dozens of witnesses besides. Maybe not Tau and his friends, but everyone else surely saw what happened and wouldn't lie. Unless they would. But why would they? I don't believe most intelligent species have a predisposition to dishonesty. Though that would be a fascinating study. Regardless, there were lots of witnesses who would surely vouch for you. Granted your use of force might have been excessive. Those last several hits when that boy fell limp especially. You know they say that happens when the damage is so extensive that the body must shut down to conserve energy. The nano are working so hard and generating so much heat that-"

"Okay," snapped Kit, stopping, "I don't want to know that. I mean, I know what I did."

Ash knit her brows, then glanced down at her feet, and said, "I'm sorry. I ramble when I get nervous."

"You must get nervous a lot," he said with a weak smile.

She returned the smile and hit him in the arm.

He nodded at her, as though to say he deserved it, and they resumed their walk to the training rooms in silence. Kit felt ashamed, for the fight, for snapping at Ash, but he felt angry too. Something about the encounter with Phlot had made him angry. Was it the threat of lashing or the mention of Bolts? He couldn't be sure.

The Mog had been a peaceful species of hunter-gatherers before they were discovered by the Masters. To hear Egg describe it, the Mog had lived in a sort of utopia of ecological balance. More vegetarian than meat eater, they worshipped trees and grass and rain and the animals of the field. After a Mog fighter emerged as the unlikely victor of the games, and the Mog ascended to citizenship, everything changed. They were rapidly industrialized, their world all but strip-mined for resources, and their society aggressively reorganized based on the Three Pillars of Imperial Hegemony. In less than four generations the Mog were transformed from gentle naturalists into the vanguard of the slaver fleets.

"You can't blame them for what they became," Egg had told him. "Even victory has a heavy price."

But Kit did blame them. He blamed the Mog and he blamed Phlot. The overseer had fought in the Al'tkash campaign, he'd said. For all Kit knew Phlot might have murdered his friend Egg.

"Hey," said Ash as they reached the training rooms. "See you after?"

"Yea," responded Kit. "I'll meet you in the mess for lunch."

She squeezed his arm where she'd hit it and turned to leave. Kit wanted to say something else to her. To apologize. To tell her all that he was feeling and all he was thinking. All the things he kept from her the night before. About Egg, and his doubts, and his dreams. But instead he just watched her go.

Kit pushed himself hard during training that morning. He ran ten extra kilometers than was his average and did extra repetitions at each of the machines. If Bolts noticed he didn't say anything about it, and made no comment about Kit's trip to the overseer's office either, though he would have definitely been informed.

Only when they sparred did his teacher say, "Anger will cloud you. Only a clear mind can win."

But did he want to win? The Mog had won and had been shaped into monsters. And to hear Ash tell it, humanity already had a tendency toward monstrosity. To lose meant slavery, but to win might mean something worse, if not for his people than for all peoples.

Lunch passed without incident. Ash spent most of the time talking about cellular decay and average life expectancy across species. Nanos had effectively tripled the natural lifespan of most life forms, she said, while having the adverse effect of slashing fertility rates. She couldn't prove anything without hard data, but she theorized that longevity minus fertility actually resulted in a cosmic net loss. Meaning most species would suffer extinction at some critical point after indoctrination, though probably not for thousands of years.

"Curiously," she said sipping on a thick protein shake, "I think the Masters are immune to the effect."

Kit had only half listened. His mind was elsewhere. Though he did notice the wild boy with the four arms staring at him from three tables away all throughout the meal.

"Well if it isn't the monkey boy," said Tau, looming above him as he and Ash stepped out from of the mess hall. "I've been hoping to run into you."

As usual Tau wasn't alone. His clique of crafted boys stood all around him, leering at Kit, with the exception of the Bluecard, who Kit had thrashed with his lunch tray. That one kept his eyes on the floor.

"What do you want, craftee," said Ash, contemptuously.

Tau kept his dark stare firmly on Kit, the pigment in his skin moving as he breathed. "I want a fight."

"You'll get one," responded Kit, straightening his back, trying to match the other boy's height as best as he could. "The games begin in a few days."

"No," said Tau, "now. In the practice arena."

It was a pointless waste of time, Kit thought. What would it prove if he won? What would it prove if he lost? Only arena combat mattered, and despite whatever Bolts might have said on the subject, Kit thought it was foolish to let his opponents know his strengths and weaknesses before the games. His one advantage was that they underestimated him, after the fight in the mess hall, maybe even feared him. But Tau meant to undo all that, to break down his moral.

"Most matches are won or lost before they even begin," Bolts had told him and then jabbed a long white finger at his head. "Here."

Fighting Ash had been one thing. It was harmless fun. Fighting Tau would be something else. A mind game, one that he had no interest in. But the unspoken rule of the barracks was that no fighter could refuse a challenge, so Kit had no choice.

"All right," he said, "I'll fight you."

Tau crossed his arms, his pigment rippling, "And I'll win."

Kit walked to his room with Ash on his heels giving him advice the whole way. She'd fought Tau on her first day at the barracks, she told him, and he'd just barely beat her. "He's hard to see," she said, "because of that pigment in his skin, but he cheats too. He kicks and punches, anything to win." That was something to admire, at least.

Back in his room Kit stripped out of his jumpsuit and pulled on his battle suit and helm. Then he found his sword, spinning the sword in his hands as though winding the blade. Ash talked at him from the doorway, and then all the way back down to the practice arena. "He has a long reach made only longer by that stupid spear of his," she said. "You have to get in close and try to knock him off balance. Maybe you can catch him when he's trying to vault? The worst thing is that blur he does when he moves. It makes you dizzy. Disoriented."

Kit listened to all she had to say but didn't respond. He already knew how to beat Tau, if not to win.

All the fighters had come out for the match, crowded around the arena floor or watching from the railing of one of the barracks' three tiers. Even the rocknid was there, standing on the west side of the arena, looking like a mountain with eyes. The excitement was understandable. There was little to do in the barracks after morning exercise, and given Tau's status as the practice champion and Kit's own notoriety from the mess hall, this was likely the most exciting thing to happen until the start of the games.

When he stepped out onto the practice arena, Tau was already there. Standing on his start pad, surrounded in green light, double bladed spear in his left hand.

"Any final words, monkey boy?" mocked Tau, the pigment swirling across his exposed chest, arms, and legs, already blurring his details slightly.

Kit only lowered his visor and took his place on his own start pad, the circle turning green as he stepped onto it. Immediately the lights brightened, washing away the rest of the barracks, the balconies, the spectators, even the bright afternoon sky above, and the computer began its countdown from ten.

Both got into start position. Kit with his sword raised to his side, both hands tight around the grip. Tau with his spear in his left hand, the shaft half resting on his forearm, his right hand extended.

...8, 7, 6...

Kit thought back to his fight with Ash the day before. About how differently it had felt than anything he'd experienced before, when fighting

Bolts or when in the fight simulator. Everything had slowed. Time seemed to stand still. But why? What had been different?

...5, 4, 3...

At first he thought it was adrenaline. Simulators, especially when played enough, are no substitute for a real, living, breathing opponent. But Kit had experiences the rush of adrenaline half a thousand times in practice with Bolts and what he experienced with Ash felt nothing like that.

...2, 1, FIGHT!

And suddenly there it was again. Slow motion, three quarters speed, maybe less. Just as before he couldn't move any faster, but his mind was there, soaking everything in.

Tau was across from him at the other edge of the arena. He hadn't moved off the start pad yet. He stood in place and swung his double bladed spear this way and that way, twirled, spun, slashed. He was performing for his audience and trying to intimidate Kit both, and it might have worked at full speed, but in the stillness the act had lost its ferocity. In fact it was quite beautiful, Kit thought.

Kit lowered his sword. And glanced up to the platforms above him, lumbering slowly through the air, the lights shining on him from above, the glass and faint blue of the sky beyond that. If he concentrated he could almost see the individual light particles, the layers of fabric that enclosed him, the space between and within atoms. Or perhaps he was dreaming? Still in bed, still in Michigan, his little brother in the bed beside him.

Tau had taken a step off his platform. He was coming for him, Kit realized. And although he was winding up to a full charge, to Kit he looked like he was barely moving. One long foot, skin, to muscle to bone, extended body to floor.

Kit let out his breath, turned his back to Tau, racing at him, and took one, two, three, four, five steps up and off the arena floor. Suddenly the lights flashed, and the computer announced: "Winner by forfeit, Tau Abravin Morsh, Ifis," announced the automated voice over the speakers. "Combat time: 8 seconds."

Tau ran another five meters before he realized what had happened. Then he stopped, looked around the arena, and finally ripped off his helmet, his face a mess of confusion and anger.

"Where are you going?" he demanded of Kit, who quietly, and purposefully was making his way back to his room. "I challenged you! You have to fight me! You have to fight me!"

But Kit didn't reply. He walked out beyond the practice arena, up one flight of steps, then another, all the while the other fighters in the barracks watching him. Some stricken by confusion, some snickering, others blank and unreadable.

"I knew you were a coward!" shouted Tau from the arena floor. "Monkey boy can't fight! Monkey boy won't fight! He's too afraid to face me! You hear that? You're afraid!"

Kit made it back to his room. He stowed his sword in one locker, his helmet and battle suit in another. Then he got back in his jumpsuit and went to the bathroom to splash some water on his face. An eight second fight where nothing had happened. So why did he suddenly feel so tired?

When he stepped back out of the washroom, Ash was there in his room waiting for him. "Why did you do that?" she asked him.

"Because I wanted to throw him off," replied Kit, "I wanted him to doubt himself."

"You fought me," she said.

"I did."

"You did."

"That was different," he replied.

"Why?"

"It was just different."

"Why?" she asked again.

"We're friends."

"That's not it."

"It's not?"

"It's because you don't see me as a threat, isn't it?" She crossed the room to where he was standing, coming to just an arm's length from him. "Do you think I can't beat you? Do you think I'm not as strong as he is? Do you think I shouldn't be taken seriously?

"You did beat me," said Kit.

"After you beat me," said Ash, anger flashing across her face.

"That was different," insisted Kit. "That was for fun. This was-"

"What? What was it?" she snapped. "This was serious? Because Tau can fight and I can't? Because I'm just some scared little girl who wouldn't possibly stand a chance if we were fighting for real?" She punched him in the chest, not hard enough to knock him down but hard enough to make him flinch. "When I learned about your species I learned all about your patriarchy. How you divide yourselves along gender lines. How you regard females as weaker. Make no mistake human, if we happen to face each other in the game I'll fight you and I'll win."

"It's not like that," he protested.

"Then what's it like?" she punched him again, harder. "What's it like?"

"I-"

"Tell me I'm wrong."

Kit tried to respond. He wanted to tell her she misunderstood. He wanted to try to explain what he meant. But Ash shook her head and stormed out before he could utter a syllable. And so he was left there, standing in his room, a dull pain in his chest where Ash had hit him, once again alone.

Chapter 6: Bragg

That night, for the first time, Kit's dream changed.

He was in his house, cream-colored walls and thick wall-to-wall carpeting. As before his dad was sprawled out on the couch in the living room, glasses on his face, reading one of his history books by the light streaming from the windows. His mom and brother were sitting at the dining room table, putting together some kind of craft project. There was a racket outside. Kit crossed the living room to the front door and turned the knob.

Out on the front lawn where a dozen workmen had usually been laboring, there stood only one. He had black skin, a heavy gut in a checkered shirt, and stubble on his face. The tools that had always been strewn about the lawn were gone, as were the generators and most of the scaffolding, save for a simple frame supporting several thick sheets of plastic, beyond which stood the mysterious construction project, now, finally complete. The crowd of onlookers that had gathered in the street and on the sidewalk had grown, and Kit noticed that it now included aliens as well.

Kit took a step out onto the stoop, another onto the path leading across the sod, and one more until he was at the elbow of the workman. Kit pulled at the man's tool belt. Once, twice, three times. The workman finally glanced down, smiled and said, "Come to see what we've built?"

Kit nodded.

The workman's smile broadened. He put his big hand on Kit's small shoulder and said, "Then what are you waiting for? Go on. Go on have a look."

Kit glanced over his shoulder and noticed his parents and little brother standing in the doorway of the house. Their faces were utterly expressionless.

Kit took a step toward the scaffolding, raising his hand to touch the plastic sheets that hung between him and whatever lay on the other side. A murmur of anticipation went through the crowd, as people shifted to see. Kit took another step, and as his fingers brushed the plastic sheeting a spark exploded from the surface. He was suddenly knocked back two meters falling hard into the grass, electricity surging, burning his fingertips and the skin of his forearm. He grabbed at it, the pain constricting his muscles and sending jolts of agony along his entire right side. As he rolled in the grass, gritting his teeth, his arm in knots, Rodney Richter and Chris Caputo appeared above him, laughing. "Useless," they said.

Kit opened his eyes, shot up and clutched his forearm. He was back in his room. Awake, in the dark. About two hours before dawn, according to the display on his screen. His arm hurt. Blinding pain, real and surging, spiking with every breath he took. It was a few seconds before the discomfort began to ease, a full minute before it was gone.

Kit stood, found the bathroom and ran the hot water in the sink. He warmed his hand and arm, and splashed some water on his face. He raised himself back up and looked in the mirror. For just an instant, he thought he saw his parents and little brother standing behind him, their faces expressionless.

After a failed attempt at more sleep, Kit went to the mess hall for some breakfast. He hoped to run into Ash, to try and explain himself again, but she wasn't there. He ate a light meal, feeling the glare from Tau from across the room, and noticed once again the four-armed wild boy staring at him throughout.

Training ran by as it usually did. Stretching, breathing, cardio, weights, resistance, fencing. Bolts was as silent as ever, wholly occupied by the update he'd made to the software that monitored Kit's daily performance, via the implant in his head. "It'll allow me to better coach you when in combat," he'd said. But Kit didn't see the point. The games were only a few days away, how much could any computer program help him now?

Kit didn't bother telling Bolts about his dream, or about the pain he'd felt in his arm. He thought it best to keep it to himself. The last thing he wanted was to be poked and prodded by the overseer, or worse, a priest. He still hadn't seen a priest in the flesh, but he knew from Egg that they presided over the games, and were always called in whenever anything out of the ordinary happened. Only in passing did Kit wonder if the pain he'd felt that night had at all registered on his trainer's monitoring software.

Kit did learn from Bolts that another two fighters had surrendered their worlds to the Masters that morning. One of them was Bluecard, the boy he'd trounced in the mess hall. The other was one of the reptilians, though Kit didn't know which one. So far that was nine less fighters that Kit would have to worry about.

"Most fighters, if they intend to forfeit their worlds, will do so just before the start of combat," Bolts told him. "It won't be on the order of the Great Kneeling, but more will drop off before the opening ceremonies."

The Great Kneeling had occurred five games past, when all forty-seven of that year's fighters forfeited out of the games and surrendered their worlds, kneeling before Lord Emperor Aejus'lobine in a dramatic act of submission. Egg had told him that the event had been staged by the Masters, as they'd decided that not one of the forty-seven worlds competing that year were worthy of citizenship. As they could not openly deny the right of combat they had instead given the fighters a choice: submit or watch your world be destroyed. All forty-seven took a knee.

At lunch Kit looked for Ash again and again was disappointed. He ate alone, sullen, only to find Tau waiting for him at the mess hall doorway after the meal was done.

"I challenge you, monkey boy," he said, his face contorted. "Practice arena. Now."

Kit went to his room. He stripped out of his jumpsuit and pulled on his battle suit and helm. Then he found his sword and walked back down to the arena. Most of the fighters had gathered to watch as they had the time before, though less of them this time, and still no Ash. After he stepped onto his start pad, the computer counted down from ten. Jolt. Slow motion. A few steady steps out of the arena. "Winner by forfeit, Tau Abravin Morsh, Ifis," announced the automated voice over the speakers. "Combat time: 7 seconds."

"You're a coward monkey boy!" screamed Tau, throwing his helmet at Kit as he raced after him across the arena. "Fight me! Fight me!"

Kit watched Tau's helmet hit the floor and spin in place a few meters from him, but did not respond.

"You're nothing!" Tau shouted angrily. "You're nothing but a coward!"

Still and silent, Kit thought as their eyes met.

Tau stopped suddenly, even taking half a step back. "Fight me damn it! You have to fight me!"

Kit glanced at the faces of the other fighters staring at him and noticed Phlot, the overseer, up on the second level. Then he turned his back on Tau and slowly walked back to his room.

As he put his battle suit and helm away he thought about Ash again. *She can't avoid me forever*, he thought. *Can she?*

With no company and little else to do, Kit decided to waste some time in a fight simulator. So, with sword in hand, he made his way back downstairs and headed toward the training rooms, but cut right into the first door he saw.

Two rows of massive black metal spheres, each perched on top of a metal pedestal and covered with glowing panels, stretched the full length of a long and dim room. The panels, Kit knew, were communicating wirelessly with a series of terminals, humming, flashing, and beeping that hung from the ceiling above.

As he made his way into the room he noticed the first three simulators nearest to the door were in use. All three spheres were moving, running, turning, spinning in a myriad of directions, at varying speeds. From inside he could hear muffled shouts and the faint echo of movement. As he walked past he could feel the floor vibrating.

Kit made his way to the fourth sphere in line and found the door open and the simulator vacant. He stepped up and in. As he entered the door automatically shut behind him and suddenly a whole new world came to life around him.

Fight simulators were actually virtual reality generators that could simulate any sight or sensation that the player could ask for, even taste and smell. They offered a 360 degree perspective, unlimited movement, and depth simulation. It was like playing no video game on Earth. Standing in a sphere with the program running, a fighter had the sensation of being anywhere but a confined space, and by virtue of the sphere's gyros and gravity wells, one could jump, and run, and kick, and fight, without ever making contact with the simulator's curved wall.

The simulator could render any environment in the known universe and generate any foe from among those already indoctrinated into the Empire. And when computer generated fighters hit, you'd feel it. Their weapons wouldn't penetrate, rather they would pass through harmlessly, but the force of impact was real enough. Kit suspected that the fight simulators could be, and probably were, used for all sorts of different things. You could conceivably generate anything inside a sphere. But fighters weren't supposed to waste time playing games, they were supposed to train, so combat was the only type of simulation allowed.

Kit was standing in an infinite white space, with no features but a thin grey line that looked to be a distant horizon. This was the simulator's lobby. A blank canvas on which anything could be built.

"Computer," he said aloud, his voice echoing into the distance. "Desert environment."

In a flash he was standing in a desert that stretched into the horizon, where a series of black mountains rose against a red sky. Above him were thin grey clouds and long tendrils of electricity, hanging down from the stratosphere, connecting like the neurons of some dying brain. Above the clouds was a moon, big and bright, cracked and splintered, filling up half the sky. Underfoot, crushed into the sand, were millions of bone fragments. They were fish mainly sometimes a bird, bleached and dried and more rock than bone. Kit had never been in this particular simulation, with an entire galaxy to choose from, billions of planets, it could be any place, any time, but even so, it looked oddly familiar.

"Computer," he said aloud, his voice carried across the sands. "Al'tkash opponent."

Standing some fifteen meters before him was materialized an Al'tkash warrior, looking much like Bolts except larger and with shorter bones coming out of the top of his head. He wore a grey battle suit and carried two short swords, one in each hand, and had a great sword strapped across his back. When Kit had first been taken he'd spent countless hours fighting simulated

Al'tkash warriors, before he'd accepted that Bolts wasn't his captor, but another captive.

"Computer," said Kit, "replace with a Mog."

Instantly the Al'tkash warrior was gone and a Mog was standing in his place, big, hairless, and bloated, he was equipped with a pair of bladed fist weapons and wore a red battle suit. He looked a lot like Phlot, the overseer, except his wooden skin was a darker shade of pink.

"Computer," said Kit, "change weapon to double bladed battle-axe."

And so instantly the Mog was holding a double bladed axe, the blades almost as large as he was. Kit crouched into a ready stance, sword up to protect his neck and head.

"Computer," he said. "Fight."

The Mog came to life. Snarling, screaming he swung his axe wildly into the air and a second later charged. Kit waited a heartbeat before doing the same. As they closed the Mog went high, his heavy battle-axe swinging down over his head. Kit could project the point of impact easily enough and went low, half sliding as he brought his sword up across his opponent's midsection. The slice was fast and true. Blood splatter. A groan. And a second later the Mog collapsed into the bones and sand.

Kit stood, brushing dirt off his jumpsuit, and frowned. "Computer, what's the difficulty setting?"

"Eight," came the reply.

"Computer, set to highest possible difficulty and increase opponent speed by thirty percent."

"Difficulty set to ten," responded the automated voice. "Opponent speed increased."

The dead Mog vanished and was brought back living and fresh, standing some fifteen meters from Kit. He held a double bladed battle-axe in his large hands.

Kit crouched again. Sword up. "Computer, fight," he said.

The Mog came at him again, though much faster, his double bladed battle-axe swinging up and over with less difficulty. Kit dodged the first swing, then turned and countered another, the force of the impact of the axe against his sword pushing him back slightly each hit. But it was still not enough. Axe and sword made contact three more times, and on his fourth swing the Mog over extended. Kit jumped and sliced down into the opening. A moment later the Mog was in the sand again, face down in a puddle of blood, his left arm severed.

Kit sighed. The fight simulator had become less and less of a challenge over the years. When he had started training first level difficulty seemed impossible, but at a certain point in his first year, Kit turned a corner, and the curve all but vanished.

"Computer, increase opponent speed to maximum."

"Opponent speed increased," came the reply.

There he stood again, fifteen meters from Kit, alive with both arms attached, battle-axe at the ready.

Kit got into position and said, "Computer, fight."

This time the Mog moved at a blazing speed. The axe blurred in his hands as he came charging, swinging with crushing strength. Kit blocked, recoiled, countered, blocked again and dodged. The Mog was on him every step, the axe sweeping down on him with unnatural rapidity, digging trenches in the sand and bone with every miss.

And yet, despite the swiftness of the attack, Kit felt calm, at ease with every step of the battle. *Still and silent*, he thought as he moved fluidly between each position, contact, block, and counter. His mind was clear, his reflexes sharp, he could almost anticipate every move his opponent was going to make. *How many times have I run this simulation?* he wondered as he swung his sword up and over, connecting with his opponent's neck.

The fight had gone less than a minute. Kit hadn't even broken a sweat. As he stared at the dead Mog, head severed, blood seeping into the desert floor, he thought about his fight with Ash and his almost fight with Tau. He thought about how everything had seemed to move in slow motion. He thought about the pain he felt in his dream and upon waking. *What's happening to me?*

Kit glanced up at the red sky and the lines of electrical current running between the thin grey clouds. He looked at the broken moon, bright aglow, and thought how much it resembled the moon he remembered from when he was just an ordinary kid living on a tree-lined street in a town in Michigan. Would he recognize his world if he went back? Would he want to go back if he could?

He stayed there in the simulation for a long while, the headless Mog beside him, thinking about his dream, about his family, and about his world.

***

His name was Bragg and Kit found him waiting outside his room when he got back upstairs from the fight simulator. As soon as Kit approached the other drew two right hands at him. After a moment of confusion, the wild boy reddened, lowering one of his arms, and declared that he and Kit were to become friends. Kit didn't see any reason to object, so he shook the other's hand and friends they became.

"I have been observing you for long time," said Bragg, "and you have impressed me."

Bragg was from a large world where the gravity was slightly stronger than it was on the capital, so that despite his robust frame he carried himself with a sort of grace that was unexpected. Though truth be told, seeing him up close and standing, the wild boy didn't look nearly as heavy or squat as he seemed the first time Kit had laid eyes on him. He was thick, for sure, but more muscle than fat, mostly on his upper half, and his four arms and two legs were surprisingly long and lean.

Bragg liked to talk almost as much as Ash except that he spoke slower and had an odd accent, despite the nano programming. Most of all he liked to make himself laugh.

"When I heard that Bluecard forfeited his world I thought that it must be first world defeated by lunch tray!" he said, roaring.

Bragg's people came in just as many cultural varieties as humans did on Earth, though were apparently not even half as quarrelsome. No wars to speak of, no major conflicts of any kind in thousands of years. Though apparently they did enjoy any and all manner of sport. Bragg himself came from a densely forested region of his planet that specialized in woodworking. He described entire cities built in the trees and of magical machines that travelled the skies between them, many hand crafted by his parents, his brothers, and sisters.

"After I go home I build cloud sails too," he said with no small amount of pride. Kit didn't bother mentioning that neither of them would probably ever see their homes. He figured Bragg knew it already anyway.

As they sat in the mess eating dinner, Ash still noticeably absent, Kit asked him why he had four arms to which Bragg replied, "Why do you have only two?"

Kit smirked as he took a morsel out of his meat pie with his fork, "That's a good point." He didn't know what kind of meat it was, and probably didn't want to.

"It is good advantage with daggers," said Bragg between bites of what could only be described as green chicken. "I trained with short swords too. Anything in close. Like working with the tools that my father had in our shop."

Kit thought about his own dad. "What is he like?" he asked.

"My father? Bigger than me. Stronger too. If he here he would carry four axes and cut everyone and the Masters to pieces." Bragg smiled, food in his teeth. "He funny too. Make you laugh all day. Tell you stories all night. I wish you could meet him."

They both sat in silence for a moment. Kit wanted to tell Bragg about his dad back on Earth. How loving he was, that he too was always there to protect and nurture him. He wanted to tell Bragg that his dad was strong and funny. But none of that was true. Kit realized he barely knew his father, rarely interacted with him at all, outside of the times when the old man would lecture him on history, on the world, on how bad people could be. "I'm preparing you for what's out there, you should listen," he'd say.

Did he miss me? Does he even care that I'm gone? Kit thought. His mom would care. His mom did miss him, he was sure of that. But it had been three years and she had his little brother to look after. If he somehow managed to get home, would she even recognize him when he came through the door?

Bragg slammed three fists on the table and declared, "I will see my father again. I will."

"How are you going to do that?" asked Kit.

"After I win, I will steal ship and go," said the other confidently.

"Oh?" asked Kit. "Do you know how to fly a ship?"

Bragg frowned and said, "No. This I cannot."

But I can, thought Kit.

"I think if you win you can do whatever you want," he said.

"Even fly ship?" asked Bragg.

"If you know how," said Kit.

Bragg frowned and waved two hands dismissively. "Make no matter," he said. "I get and I fly. How hard can it be. Computer do everything anyhow. So?"

"So," agreed Kit with a smile.

Bragg took another bite of his green chicken and said "You see World Ship?"

Kit shook his head no.

"I see World Ship when coming to capital," said Bragg gravely. "As large as planet. Larger than even Motherships."

"Motherships?" asked Kit.

"You not see Motherships?" asked Bragg, surprised. "They orbit this planet. Three, maybe four. At night you can see, orbiting in distance. Each must have a billion in crew. World ship, twice, three times that. Maybe that's the ship I steal?"

"I think that might prove hard," said Kit.

"I tell you, it easier than beating that one." Bragg gestured toward Tau, sitting several tables away with his lackeys. "He is a like a gow cat, hard to see, hard to focus."

"Is that why you think you lost?" asked Kit.

Bragg flushed and shook his head, "He can be seen, but his skin makes one dizzy. And he's strong, fast, hard."

"He's not so tough," said Kit, taking another stab at his pie. "You only lost because you let him get to you. When you get angry you lose."

Bragg sipped some water and asked, "Did your trainer teach you this? The Al'tkash?"

"Does everyone know about my trainer?"

"He teach you."

"He taught me a lot," agreed Kit, surprised by how true the statement really was.

Bragg nodded and said, "My trainer tell me much about your Al'tkash. One of the best fighters there ever was. Unmatched. He say he won his games, but lost due to disqualification." He studied Kit's face a moment. "By your look I think he never tell you."

Kit quickly looked down at his tray. It was true, Bolts had never told him. But of course Bolts never really told him much of anything outside of combat and training.

"He not say much," continued Bragg, "which is why I think you not say much. Al'tkash got your tongue! No?"

Bragg laughed at his own joke while Kit thought about Bolts. He knew that his trainer had been a formidable fighter. He knew also that after the games his trainer's world was nearly destroyed, most of its population murdered. The few survivors enslaved. Kit had always thought it happened when Bolts lost in the arena, but had he actually won?

"Why did he get disqualified?" he asked Bragg.

The other took another bite of his green chicken, and as he chewed said, "It is not known. Only that he was, and afterward for many, many years he was missing, many thought dead. Until now." He pointed at Kit with a grizzled, green drumstick. "Until you."

Kit tensed. "Me?"

Bragg frowned at him. "He pick you. Like my trainer pick me."

Kit pushed his tray away, "What do you mean he picked me?"

Bragg's frown grew deeper. "Masters pick worlds, but trainers pick fighters," he said, as though Kit should already know. "Your trainer choose you to fight for your world. It is why you are here."

For Kit it felt like everything fell away. Bragg was still talking, but Kit couldn't hear him. There were still others in the mess hall, sitting at the tables around them, but Kit couldn't see them.

It had always been Bolts. The reason Kit was there, the reason he'd been chosen. Why he'd been taken from his parents, and little brother. All that time it had been Bolts. Always Bolts. And he'd always known it. All his dismissals, and evasions, of course it was him.

"You're here, what does it matter?" he'd said.

What was he feeling? Anger? Betrayal? Hurt? *Still and silent,* he thought, and immediately resented himself for falling back to his training.

As his mind raced he had only the faint awareness that he rose from his seat, that Bragg was shouting after him, that Tau and his lackeys were mocking him. He was only vaguely conscious of leaving the mess hall, crossing the barracks and rushing past the training rooms and fight simulators through the doors leading to the trainers' dorm. And when he found Bolts, sitting on the floor of his room, legs crossed, face caste downward in meditation, Kit was only mildly cognizant of rushing him, of kicking and punching at him, of screaming and wanting only to hurt him. To kill him. To make him feel all that Kit had suppressed and hidden away for three long years.

The Al'tkash trainer did not fight back. He took each hit, unflinching, unmoving, blood darkening his skin and just as quickly disappearing as the nano did their work. Only when he could did he grab Kit's arms to restrain him, brought him close and held him. Held him until Kit's fury turned to anguish, until his rage turned to sadness. Until he stopped thrashing, and kicking and only shuddered with grief, repeating, "you picked me," between labored breaths. He wanted to cry, but no tears came.

Bolts held him tight for a long time before finally saying, "I should have told you. I'm sorry." Then he stood, raising Kit in his arms, and placed him gently on the bed, laying a hand on the boy's head, before returning to his spot on the floor. For a long time they sat in silence.

"After my victory I refused ascension," said Bolts finally, his dark eyes on Kit, his face blank. "I did not wish to see my people become brutal, like the Mog, like the others. For this insult I was disqualified and sent to Ud'Na for punishment and reeducation, while my world was destroyed."

He took a long silent breath. "After many long years, once I was deemed rehabilitated, I was commanded to be a trainer. As all vanquished fighters not deemed worthy of becoming gladiators must become. As a gesture of graciousness, the Masters allowed me first pick among the new worlds they planned to conquer." He stared deeply into Kit's eyes, "I chose Earth. And after a prolonged study, I chose you."

"Why me?" asked Kit, his head pounding, his chest tight.

"There were multiple factors," his trainer replied, "but above all of them, I chose you because you are special."

Kit clenched his jaw. "Special? How?"

Bolts seemed to consider the question, or perhaps what his answer ought to be, and after a moment said, "The milkwomen believe that the gods set the rolls." He raised a brow. "There's truth in that."

Chapter 7: Practice

Kit twisted his hands around the grip of his sword, his knuckles bare white, as the voice of the game computer counted down from ten. In front of him, at the other end of the practice arena stood Tau, his spear in his hand, splayed across his arm.

...8, 7, 6...

Kit was thinking about his opening move, considering if it was better to charge or wait for the other's attack. The platforms were moving counterclockwise around the arena, just above their heads. It be easy enough to grab one and ride it to close the distance. There were also the gravity wells. These were more unpredictable, but unpredictable could be good.

...5, 4, 3...

He cleared his mind. *Nothing but the fight*, he thought. There was no use in overthinking it. He'd let Tau set the opening. He'd read him. Predict him. And respond. Bolts had taught him to take his time. Other fighters, especially bigger fighters, would underestimate him, come at him quickly, aggressively. They'd spend their energy, reveal their weaknesses, open themselves up to attack. *Watch. Study. Attack.*

..2, 1, FIGHT!

Over the last three days a sort of routine had established itself.

After a quick breakfast, sometimes with Bragg, sometimes alone, Kit trained with Bolts as he always had, but now a new kind of tension hung between them. Every morning Kit felt the urge to ask Bolts more questions, to explain more of what he'd meant and what he meant for him to do, but every morning Kit decided to stay silent.

He was angry, that much he knew, but he was also aware that if it hadn't been him it might have been someone else and his home and his family would still be in danger. He also knew there was nothing to be done now. He was there, days away from combat, there was no going back. And yet what nagged him most was the guilty feeling that he didn't care at all, about any of it.

Lunches were spent with Bragg, the wild boy telling jokes and stories of his home. Immediately followed by yet another confrontation by Tau. Another challenge. Another forfeit.

Afternoons were spent in the fight simulator. Max difficulty. Max speed. Kit dispatched his opponents with brutal efficiency. And then would linger in the simulator, visiting alien worlds, dreaming of being free. Then dinner with Bragg in the evening, then to his room and bed. Every night his dream was the same. His dad reading. The project finished. Electrical discharge. Pain.

Three days passed this way. In that time Kit managed to catch Ash half a dozen times, twice in the simulator room, twice coming out of training, once in the mess hall, once on her way to her room. He spoke to her every time. He tried explaining to her why he didn't want to fight Tau. But every time she told him, "If you won't fight him, then I have nothing to say to you."

Six more fighters forfeited their worlds to the Masters in those three days. A ruddy hominid from a world called Yu'son. A yellow skinned Avager. A fat Oblox called Toolo. A cat-like Veercan. A tall, graceful insectoid from a world called Darkspear. A craftee with pale skin and bright green eyes who someone had nicknamed Clip.

And always there was the waiting. Waiting on the games to begin. For real combat to start and the fate of thirty-two remaining worlds to be decided.

On the fourth day everything changed.

Kit heard the commotion before he stepped into the mess hall. Shouting. A chair sliding across the floor. Trays falling.

Everyone was on their feet. The insectoids and reptillians, the enormous rocknid, the bestial Optwap, Bragg. They were all watching a confrontation, about to be a fight, at the center of the room, where Tau and his nine remaining craftees stood surrounding someone short, or down on the floor.

"I say we beat her until her brain shuts down," said one of Tau's minions with a sneer.

"Try it and I'll take your eyeball out of your skull," came the reply.

Kit recognized the voice immediately.

"Maybe we should lash her like the Masters do to bad slaves," said another of the craftees, "she might as well get used to it."

Kit shoved past an eel-skinned creature with white on white eyes called a Blight, and as he did a couple of the craftees noticed him, one of them saying, "Hey look, it's her boyfriend, the monkey."

"Leave her alone," demanded Kit as he got to them.

Tau turned and pushed him back with such force that Kit fell backward into a table. As breakfast trays crashed to the floor the craftees laughed, Tau most of all, before he asked, "What are you gonna do coward? We both know you're just gonna run away like you always do." They laughed louder.

There was no way he could fight ten of them. Even if Ash and Bragg both joined in to help, as he hoped they would, they'd still be outnumbered. And the craftees were bigger and stronger besides. Whatever peace he'd enjoyed after his fight with the Bluecard was gone. They'd attack and make him hurt. His only chance was to fight Tau one on one, and luckily he knew how to provoke him.

"I challenge you," said Kit, as he raised himself back to his feet. "In the arena. Now."

Tau let out a laugh and said, "Why? So that you can forfeit again monkey boy?"

"No. Not this time," said Kit. "I'll fight you. And I'll beat you."

The craftees laughed, and Tau said, "You're lying. You'll forfeit."

Kit smirked. "Who's the coward now?"

You could hear a pin drop in the mess hall.

Tau's face darkened. "In the arena," he said. "Ten minutes."

"Ten minutes," Kit agreed.

After Tau shouldered past Kit, and the other craftees dispersed, Kit walked up to Ash, who was sitting down on the floor, and offered her his hand.

"I can take care of myself," she said at him angrily.

"Against one, or two, or three, I don't doubt it. Not against ten. Not alone," he said. "I wouldn't have stood a chance either."

She scowled at him and his open hand, then relaxed her face, sighed, and let him help her up.

"I hope you know what you are doing," said Bragg as he approached them. "It will hurt. Believe me."

"I know what I'm doing," responded Kit, wondering if he would be able to carry that confidence with him.

The sun was just rising over the capital. The glass spires of the city scraped a cloudless blue sky. Enormous birds, flying creatures, and spacecraft rising to the thin lip of the atmosphere, created shadows that fell over the dome of the coliseum and the glass ceiling of the barracks like snow. But below, in the practice arena, there was only light, pure, bright, and unbroken. And as Kit stepped off the start pad to face Tau, sword in hand, everything moved so slowly, that he thought that if he looked hard enough, he could make out particle waves of photons speeding toward all things around him.

Kit knew that he wasn't moving any faster, but he was certainly thinking faster. What else could it be? The world was half frozen around him and he could stop and consider every detail of it for what seemed like an eternity. The platforms. The gravity wells. Tau, the pigment in his skin leaving him half blurred, swinging his double bladed spear as he charged. What did this mean?

Tau moved with a fury. Determined to run him down, spear point into the chest, and he meant to do it quickly. All eyes were on them. The fighters. The overseer. Even several of the trainers. Even Bolts.

Kit moved off his pad, but stood, feet planted, sword raised, ready to take the assault. At Kit's level of awareness, Tau's main biological advantage was muted. He still blurred. His details were hard to focus, but there was little power in the effect that Kit had glimpsed and Bragg described. In fact, as Kit watched Tau charge, he noticed that the older boy's movements were a little clumsy, his steps slightly uneven, his swing overly wide. But there was no question of his strength and speed. Tau was like a wild animal, fury on two legs.

"An opponent's perceived advantage is also their greatest weakness," Bolts had told him. "Because they will rely on it at the cost of everything else."

Kit's advantage was that he was underestimated. By Tau, by the Bluecard in the mess hall, by the bullies at school, by his dad. It went with his size, his tendency to be quiet, to think more than he spoke. Kit's weakness was that he also underestimated himself. *Because if I can*, he reasoned, *why is everyone else so convinced that I can't?*

Tau charged. The gap between them closed rapidly. Forty-five meters became forty, then thirty-five, then thirty. Kit stood his ground. Sword firm in his hands. He could see every movement. Every sweep of the spear, the two blades shining in the light. The dust particles drifting through the air between them. The wide eyes of the spectators, hands on the railing. But all he could hear was his own heartbeat. Slow and steady. Beat in. Beat out. Beat in. Beat out. Twenty-five meters. Twenty meters. Fifteen. Ten.

His mind drifted to his little brother. His little brother never underestimated him. Argued with him, yes. Took his stuff, always. But not once did he underrate him. Most often they relied on one another, for strength and reassurance, for alliance against their dad's harshness. He was a harsh man, Kit remembered. He demanded a lot, returned little. As black as the world he painted for them. And afraid. Perpetually afraid of everything. Three years and Kit had nearly forgotten.

Tau closed the last ten meters and brought his spear up and over in a great arc over his head and to his left, swinging down, and back up as he ran. From a distance it looked almost beautiful. Blurred lines, and glimmering hypnotic steel.

"There were these kids at my school who used to pick on me," Kit had told Egg in stasis. "My dad used to tell me never to fight them. To just let them do what they wanted and never fight back."

"Because you could lose?" asked Egg.

Kit shook his head, "Because I could win."

Tau's blade made contact with Kit's sword, the impact so strong that Kit had to brace himself to keep his balance. The spear recoiled, swung again in the other direction, Kit countered again. And again. Three more times. Four. Tau was strong, very strong. That strength along with his speed and the dizzying effects of the pigment in his skin could devastate most any fighter in the barracks. But in slow motion Tau seemed mistimed and ungainly. His pigment little else than a curious decoration. And Kit saw something else. In Tau's face and eyes he could see uncertainty, growing with every strike countered and swing missed.

Kit blocked, pushed back, swung, blocked again. It became a rhythm, unconscious and quickening. The barracks spun around them and exploded into flame until there was nothing left but the clash of metal and the sound of Kit's heart. Beat in. Beat out. Beat in. Beat out. And in the center there was only stillness and Kit's quick mind. Watching, analyzing, predicting, reacting.

This was different from before. Different than his fight with Ash, different than his abortive fights with Tau. He felt removed from himself. Out of body. More spectator than fighter. And as he watched his mind whirled with frustration at his own languidness. He couldn't move any faster but he thought he should move faster. He knew he could move faster and yet, nothing.

Tau swung wildly over Kit's head, then sidestepped to the left, then again to the right. Kit realized that he was trying to increase his blur. He wanted to disorient him, as he'd done with all his other opponents. But it wouldn't work now, it couldn't work. Not with Kit. At every point he mirrored Tau's movement, met his blades and pushed inside his reach. Again and again, forcing Tau to step back, try to increase his distance. Kit would counter, dodge, block, and take another step.

Tau was, Kit thought, a better fighter than this, but he didn't know how to compensate for someone who could look past his primary advantage.

Tau pushed back, blade to sword, took a step back and used his spear to pivot ninety degrees. Kit immediately moved to match, landing on a gravity well a meter away just as Tau fell into a sprint. Up into the air, twenty meters, and Kit shot across a third of the arena in a narrow arc that dropped him directly in his opponent's path. Tau saw too late, but to his credit dropped his spear to vault over Kit as he made touchdown. His aim was off. Kit raised his sword and caught the spear mid shaft.

Tau landed with a crash and slid another ten meters before he stopped. Kit was on him a moment later. They met with an explosion of violence. Block. Counter. Block. Counter. Their hypnotic blades sparked as they fought and scraped. Block. Counter. Block. Counter. And for a moment in that rhythm, in the automation of the fight, Kit thought he glimpsed a string connecting everything. Connecting his dad and his mom, his little brother and the bullies in school, Bolts and the Masters, Ash, Bragg, even Tau. A line flowing out of him and into everything that ever was or ever could be. Beyond this world beyond all worlds. Beyond even the universe.

Tau jumped back to his feet. He found his rhythm again. He swung. Kit blocked. He swung. Kit countered. Back and forth. Again and again. Seconds into minutes. Minutes into full rotations of the clock. They clashed again so hard that both lost their weapons, sword and spear went flying.

Tau screamed. Frustration. Rage. He pounced on Kit and they were on the floor, both unarmed, swinging, grappling. Kit felt Tau's hands around his throat. His eyes wild. Could the nano save him from this?

And suddenly it was over. Phlot, the overseer, appeared above them, first pulling Tau to his feet, then Kit. Grabbing each by the back of his neck with his thick heavy hands.

"You want to tear each other apart?" he shouted. "You want to kill each other? Then save your strength!" He looked up at the various fighters staring down at them from around the barracks. "THAT GOES FOR ALL OF YOU! The games begin tomorrow!" He let go of both Tau and Kit, giving each a firm shove as he did. "Go to your rooms. Go!"

Slowly the other fighters began to disperse. Murmurs between them. Kit noticed Bolts up on the third level. His trainer looked at him, his face as expressionless as ever, and turned to walk away.

Kit turned to Tau, seething a few steps away.

Kit was about to try and say something, anything, but before he could the other boy snarled, "I don't know what you are. But when I see you in combat, I'll kill you."

Kit watched Tau retrieve his spear and walk away.

"No one else might appreciate your victory," came a familiar voice. "But I do."

Kit smiled and turned to face Ash. "It wasn't a victory."

"You didn't let him beat you," she said. "That counts as a win. Maybe not in the coliseum, but here it does."

"So I take it you're talking to me again?" he asked.

"I realized that without me you're prone to get into all sorts of trouble," she replied.

He wanted to hug her, but stayed where he was.

"Don't worry about them," she said gesturing to the upper floors. "They didn't appreciate your fight because some of them will have to face you. Like It's true what I heard about your kind. Now they all know it too. Though you'd think the lunch tray was enough. Curious how some species fail to learn the most obvious lessons even when presented with the facts multiple times. Don't you think? But no one will underestimate you after what they saw here."

Kit frowned and said, "That's what I was worried about."

She looked at him, puzzled, then said, "Is that why you wouldn't-"

"No," he said quickly. "Not really. You were right. About why I didn't want to fight Tau. About not taking you seriously. But that's because you're my friend. I'm sorry. I'm really sorry."

She studied him for a moment then suddenly hit him in the arm. "Apology accepted."

Kit winced and said, "You know, you're a better fighter than him."

"Oh, I know," she said with a smirk.

Chapter 8: Games

The matchups were posted the next morning on a large screen hanging above the massive gold doors leading to the Hall of Champions. The thirty-two remaining fighters were divided evenly into two brackets of sixteen, one white, and one black. It was a single-elimination tournament, with an optional wildcard melee and a final round between colors. Officially the matchups were randomized, but Kit suspected that nothing about the games was done at random.

"Looks like we're opposing colors," said Ash as they stood examining the board.

Kit was on the black side of the board, Ash on the white. "Maybe we won't have to fight each other at all," he said.

She looked at him sidelong and said, "Why? Are you not planning on getting to the final round? Because I am."

He snickered, but realized she was serious.

"This is for everything," she told him. "No more games. No more practice. Just combat. The winner gets ascension, the loser enslavement."

He studied her for a moment and said, "I don't believe you'd want to be like the Masters."

She frowned. "Better to be a master than to be a slave. I didn't make up the rules, but I'll play by them. I have no choice and neither do you. Would you want to see your people in chains?"

No, but the alternative might be worse, he thought, then said, "I don't think the Masters use chains."

"No," agreed Ash. "They brainwash species into thinking that servitude is the greatest honor in the entire universe. We've all been through it. In the propaganda vids and education simulation. Three years of being told how wonderful it is to submit. Most of the other fighters might be fooled but I'm not. And neither should you be. "

Kit raised his hands, "I know. I know."

"Most don't," she said, then saddened. "It takes a lot to resist."

Kit thought about Egg.

That evening the fighters donned their battle suits, without helmets or weapons. Sixteen in black. Sixteen in white. And formed two lines, led by Phlot, flanked by their trainers. The massive rocknid bringing up the rear.

Then, at the appointed hour, for the first time since their arrival, the doors to the Hall of Champions opened before them. On the other side a long corridor bathed in blue light.

"Fighters!" announced Phlot, himself dressed in an ornate red battle suit, which Kit thought was probably ceremonial. "Today you stand before the Lord Emperor himself. Know your place! Conduct yourself with honor! Savor the moment for it is the greatest of your lives!" And with those words Phlot turned toward the Hall and they began to walk. One hundred thirty feet echoing against the metal walls of the corridor, that of the rocknid loudest of all, the creature stooping as he went.

The Hall of Champions sloped down then up, the ceiling curving so that it was impossible to see the end of the tunnel. Every few meters were columns, encircled by blue light, and between the columns weapons hung in nooks in the wall. Kit wasn't sure if they were the weapons of former fighters or purely decorative, but every one was made of hypnotic steel, and every one looked to have been used.

No one spoke as they walked. Even Ash who was walking beside Kit in the white line, kept her eyes on the fighter ahead of her, daring not to betray her nerves. And although Kit wanted to say something, he realized he couldn't think of anything appropriate. They were all nervous. Even Tau, three fighters back in the black line, who had been avoiding him since the previous morning, looked unsteady.

For the first time it hit Kit, what Ash had said: this was it. This was for everything. Three years, the loss of his family and his home, never ending drills, training, simulations, had all led up to this. Fight and win, or lose everything.

As they got to the midway point in the tunnel, to the lowest point in the slope, Kit heard something above the echo of their boots. Faint at first, just a low rumble. But with every step it got louder and louder. Like a freight train coming down the track. It was a clamor so loud that one third of the way up the floor plates were vibrating. Another third and Kit could feel the noise in his bones.

Suddenly, two golden doors, the twins of those they had entered, flew open ahead of them. A light exploded into the dark tunnel with such force that Kit instinctively raised his arms to shield his eyes. A millisecond later the roar of three hundred thousand screaming voices assaulted his ears. Blind and deaf he stumbled forward, trusting his instincts over his senses.

Only after a few long moments was he able to open his eyes and found himself standing at the far end of an enormous three tiered stadium, with a glass dome and massive screens that appeared to be suspended in midair high above them. And all around were aliens, ascended species, Kit realized, hundreds of thousands of them. Some slaves moved among them too, as did a few droids, but mainly it was the slavers. Crafted largely, but among them too some Mog, some Tri-Cor, Nie'Buka, Suul-Manee, Berserkers, and of course, Masters, glowing silver from their veins. Tens of thousands of Masters, the rulers of the galaxy, in the flesh.

It took a minute for the fighters to realize that Phlot was screaming at them to get back into formation. Then it took another two for everyone to regain their bearings and resume the march, mainly because the giant rocknid was so overwhelmed by the sight of the coliseum that he kept wandering away in a daze.

Finally, they managed to cross the arena floor and arrange themselves into two long lines, one black, one white, in front of a great pavilion built into the stands. It was assembled from eight columns and draped over by a gold and silver canopy of what looked like starlight, but was actually a mesh of silver leaves. Under each of the eight columns stood a golden-armored Champion, a Master warrior, each only distinguishable by their ornate helms, each in the form of a bestial skull. And at the center of the pavilion, splayed across several ornate couches and cushioned benches, sat the royal court, with Lord Emperor Aejus'lobine at the forefront.

For a long time nothing happened. The crowd cheered. The clamor rising to the very vault of the dome and back down onto the fighters standing quietly on the white arena floor. While the imperial court chit-chatted amongst themselves, seemingly oblivious to what went on around them.

The Lord Emperor looked much like he had in Ms. Moffat's display in stasis. He was tall and slender like all Masters, twice the scale of the average human being. He had strong aquiline features, a sharp nose, and boney cheeks, with nary a hair on his head. His silver veins glowed from beneath his blue tinted skin. He wore a white, richly embroidered tunic, and over that a white jacket with silver accents and platinum epaulettes. On his head was a cobalt circlet, fashioned with eight carved, glimmering, silver spikes that rose up and bent back down into his scalp. But it was his dark eyes that drew Kit's attention.

As the Lord Emperor chatted amiably with a fearsome, masked Master in an ostentatious military uniform, lounging to his left, his eyes burned with cold disdain. Not so much for the fighters in the arena, who the Lord Emperor seemed not even to notice, but for the hundreds of thousands of cheering spectators, his adoring subjects.

As the roar finally began to quiet, a female Master appeared at the far right of the pavilion. She wore only a fitted, hooded, silver robe, aglow with writing along the seams and edges that Kit recognized as the sacred language of the clergy. As she raised her hand, which to Kit looked wrong somehow, a sudden hush fell over the coliseum. And as she began to speak her voice was at once everywhere, full, and commanding.

"Citizens," she said, her hood obscuring her face, "on behalf of Lord Emperor Aejus'lobine, victor at the Battle of the Four Pillars, conqueror of the Highborne, builder of the World Ship, blessed protector, great master, wise father, I welcome you to these centennial games!"

A roar went up from the crowd, even more deafening than what had come before.

"As we have been entrusted by the gods with the charge of infinite worlds," continued the priestess when the outcry subsided, "so too these thirty-two fighters have been consigned to represent their worlds before us. The vanquished will know the honor of servitude, while the victor will taste the fruit of ascension!"

ASCENSION! ASCENSION! ASCENSION! the crowd chanted.

Most of the fighters were looking around nervously. Even the craftees had lost their swagger. But Kit kept his gaze firmly on the priestess, who after a time raised her hand again and announced, "To the gods we give all praise! Epheus d'Aron, great father, nurturer of machines, unifier of tribes, conqueror of the stars, first among them! May he watch over us now and anoint these fighters that stand before us in blood. And through their combat may we find a singular species, one worthy of ascension from among the savage breeds. May they rise and conquer! For Duty, Unity, and Obedience!"

ASCENSION! ASCENSION! ASCENSION! the crowd chanted again.

The priestess suddenly raised her head and arms to the dome of the coliseum, and as she did Kit got his first real look at her face. She was a Master no doubt, silver glowing veins, and blue skin just like the others, but her eyes were pure white and her skin looked lined and ancient. She was old, very old, but not aged the way a human might be. She looked more like a statue, cracked and weathered.

"Gods hear our prayers!" She shouted, her voice booming over everything.

Just then, in the air above them, balls of flame erupted as though out of nowhere. Growing in size and intensity, they spun forming and arranging into systems, and galaxies, and clusters, exploding, dancing, combining and splitting, until all the open space in the coliseum was awash in flame. These weren't fireworks, Kit knew, this was the nano.

"Bless us! Bless us! Bless us!" she cried. "Bless our Lord Emperor. Bless our Empire. Bless a victor from the fighters that stand before us. And in turn we will honor you with thirty-one worlds to serve and toil until the stars cool and darkness reigns once more. All this we ask!"

The crowd went wild.

After the invocation, after Kit and the others were seated in a special box on the lip of the arena floor, it was Bolts who whispered, "The most skilled Masters can manipulate the nano in air, in water, even in other beings."

Egg had told him about whole sectors of primitive worlds that worshipped the Masters as gods for their ability to manipulate the elements. Some Masters only occasionally played the part of deity as a sort of recreation, while others set themselves up on primitive planets for hundreds, even thousands of years, allowing indigenousness species to build whole religions around them.

Dancing and acrobatics were next. Slaves from two-dozen worlds performed for the pleasure of the Lord Emperor. Spider limbed Dakurak bounced twenty meters in the air doing somersaults. Eyeless Palia juggled plasma balls that they themselves secreted. A Bavo rode a skin lion, one handed.

But the main event that evening was combat. First between former fighters turned slave gladiators, and later by the Empire's prized Champions, sent into the arena against condemned prisoners. While the gladiators, usually evenly matched, fought for long stretches, combat involving Champions lasted mere seconds.

It was true, everything that Kit had ever been told, by Egg and by Bolts, the Champions were fast, faster than fast. They moved at near light speed, so that they would seem to suddenly vanish from one position only to appear near instantaneously at another. And when they struck the condemned they'd kill, the prisoners sliced and bleeding before they could take more than a step off their start pad.

Speed was the only way to disrupt the nano, but it was also the nano that made the Champions so fast in the first place. Whether by design or luck of genetics, only the Masters possessed such powers.

All told thirty-two living beings died this way during the opening ceremonies, one for each of the thirty-two worlds remaining in the competition.

The arena floor was a pool of blood, of various colors and consistencies. It was beautiful in its grotesquery.

"Has anyone ever won against a Champion?" Kit had asked Egg in stasis.

"According to the history, no," his friend replied. "But history isn't truth, it's just what those in power tell those of us who have no power."

"So what is the truth?" asked Kit.

"The truth is that Champions are able to manipulate the nano in such a way that they can move at incredible speed, or more accurately, are able to momentarily step out of normal space-time."

"But can they be beaten?" asked Kit. "Has anyone ever done it?"

"There is a story," said Egg, "a very old story about a Master who went to a small blue primitive planet at the edge of the galaxy. He set himself up as a god and for a thousand years ruled as a wrathful deity. Until one day the native people rose up against him. He sent a Champion to put down the rebellion. Many died, until one day a young shepherd boy appeared and challenged the Champion to single combat."

"What happened?"

"He threw a rock so fast and so hard that it knocked the Champion flat on the ground," replied Egg. "Before the Champion could get back to his feet the boy was on him with his own sword. According to the story he cut the Champion's head off and delivered it to the false god."

"What did the Master do?"

Egg hesitated. "He rained fire down onto the planet and left."

"Why?"

"Because what the shepherd boy did was supposed to be impossible."

"But it is possible," said Kit.

"If you believe the story," agreed Egg.

"How did he do it?"

"He was able to use the nano the same way that the Masters do."

"But I thought it was a primitive world," said Kit.

"It was," agreed Egg.

"Then how was the nano there?"

"The nano exist in all the worlds of the Empire, in the water, in the air, in all the subjects of the Masters, in the Masters themselves. Self-replicating machines that spread like a virus the moment the Masters land on a new world."

"So the Masters don't control the nano?" asked Kit.

"No," said Egg, "they only manipulate it."

"And others can too," said Kit. "Like the shepherd boy?"

"If you believe the story," agreed Egg.

After the spectacles and combat ended a hush fell over the coliseum as the Lord Emperor rose to his feet. He straightened his jacket, and moved slowly to the edge of the pavilion, the two Champions closest to him following him out. He surveyed the crowds, smiled faintly, and cleared his throat, then he began to speak.

"Citizens," he said, his voice cold and crisp. "I welcome you. I welcome you. I welcome you all to our capital, and to these centennial games. And in the coming days I hope you find joy, and excitement, and reward, but above all I challenge you to remember why we're here." He glanced down at the floor for a moment, as though lost in thought, the audience silent. "The universe is vast and filled with emptiness. It is filled with peril and terror. It is filled with endless black. But among the countless dead worlds and dead systems, and even dead sectors, among the noxious gases and radiation and anomalies, there is life. Precious, and finite, and so very fragile." He put his hands together. "I remind you that we are entrusted by the gods to protect life. To act as loving, nurturing, and yes, sometimes stern parents." A chuckle ran through the crowd. "And although these games are part spectacle, they exist primarily to help us elevate those living beings strong enough, pure enough, worthy enough to be called citizens. For although the blessings of servitude may at times sting, the burdens of parenthood weigh heaviest.

"Victory is responsibility," he said, the faint smile still on his lips. "Responsibility to peace, and expansion, and to all our many children. Because without us there would be no peace. Only decay, and death, and emptiness. The black would rule and light would vanish from the cosmos. Only silence. Only silence. Only silence." He paused for a few moments. Not one of the three hundred thousand beings gathered stirred. "Citizens and friends, I welcome you to these sacred games. This right of passage. This entertainment." He looked to the fighters, one line black, the other white. "Fighters, your struggle will be long and hard. You will feel pain. You will feel disappointment. Many of you will fall." He placed a hand on his chest, "But one of you will rise to the challenge. One of you will prove yourself mighty. One of you will feel the light of the gods. And in your victory you shall have rewards everlasting." He threw his arms wide, "Let the games begin!"

The roar that followed shook the very foundations of the coliseum.

***

It was Bragg's idea, but Ash was the one who convinced Kit to do it. And so once the opening festivities were over, and after Phlot marched them all back to the barracks, the three fighters donned their jumpsuits and snuck out into the dark streets of the capital. Right past the Durg at the entrance. No one tried to stop them. No guards or locked doors barred their way. They simply left.

"Is something wrong?" asked Ash as they made their way down the broad empty Boulevard of Battle that led from the coliseum to the center of the city.

Kit glanced over his shoulder, half expecting to see the overseer chasing after them, then replied, "I just never thought to leave."

Ash smirked at him, "Slaves don't run away. Where would they go? No money. No ship. No destination. It's curious how we accept our lot. Another universal trait?" She put her arm through his, tugging at him. "Besides we'll be back soon. Don't you want to have some fun before tomorrow?"

He smiled back at her. He did. He wanted to have fun more than anything.

At night the streets of the capital city were awash in bright, dancing lights. Homes, shops, restaurants, all glowed red, yellow, blue, and white. Every surface was a screen, and on those screens an infinitesimal stream of strange and exciting images. Pictures both fantastical and incomprehensible. Ads, announcements, warnings. A thousand thousand civilizations pouring their collective knowledge onto the sidewalk like water out of a bucket. And with the sights were sounds, music, tones, voices filling the hot, humid air. Some whispered in Kit's ear, others boomed at him creating a cacophony so disruptive that he had to strain to keep his thoughts straight.

"Look up, up!" said Bragg, pointing three arms up over his head.

Kit looked up and saw glass, and steel, and grass, and wood rising a mile into the air above him. The spires of the Masters dominated the entire skyline. At night they rippled with light just like everything else. Flashing a rainbow of colors. And above the spires were the bright lights of starships. Some breaking the atmosphere on their way in, others breaking the atmosphere on their way out. And above them the outlines of orbital stations, and motherships, and the twin moons Ameth and Thema.

After half a kilometer they descended from the Boulevard of Battle to Market Row, where merchants from hundreds of worlds had set up their stalls. Most were slaves, owned by the large trading houses, brought to the capital to hock wares from their home worlds. A few were ascended species, trying to make a buck off the ever-fickle tourist trade. All were loud, and screaming, and fighting bloody against an army of street priests and sim dealers for the attention of those walking past.

The smells in Market Row were stronger than anything Kit had ever experienced. Stronger than the antiseptic cleanliness of the barracks or the metallic stench of the coliseum. Here was every smell imaginable, ranging from sweet right through to rancid. At once he could smell the bouquet of fresh flowers and the sour stink of rotting flesh. The musky odor of shellfish, mixed equally with the piney fragrance of cut wood. The smells from the stalls and the many alien species stormed and overwhelmed his olfactory senses until nothing remained but the faint scent memories of his mom's morning coffee and his dad's aftershave.

As they walked through Market Row, up toward the Slave Pits, the three fighters got inquisitive stares. One monstrous Berserker going even so far as to make a grab for Bragg, but the shadows of night and the crush of the crowds helped to conceal them, and propelled them onward. Three exotic species amongst a press of exotic species. Largely they were ignored. Saved mainly, perhaps, by their own ignorance.

Ash wanted to stop at every stall. To see, and feel, and taste. She laughed at a display of luminous butterflies, when one of the glowing insects fluttered against her cheek. She recoiled when a merchant offered her a sample of something that looked like month-old cow's milk and smelled three times worse. She jumped with joy at the sight of an artist who created floating sculptures out of incandescent gas.

But Bragg's insistence and the force of the crowd kept them moving forward. Further into the heart of the market and all that lay beyond.

"Step right up! Step right up!" shouted a fat Suul-Manee with typical blood red eyes and spotted skin. "Finest slaves in the cluster! Young ones, old ones, males, females, and everything in between!" He was standing up on a platform, an odd assortment of aliens with downcast eyes arranged in a row behind him. "If we don't have it you don't want it. Finest selections in the universe!"

Ash pushed against Kit and said, "I don't think we should be here."

Kit could see Bragg using all his hands to try and shove a path clear for them, but it was of no use. The throng was too thick. For the moment they were stuck.

"Here we go, here we go, here we go!" shouted the slaver as a tall, delicate, sand-skinned alien, with deep set eyes and faint ridges on her nose and ears, dressed only in a simple tunic, was shoved up onto the platform. "This exquisite creature is called a Folta and can be yours for a starting bid of just one hundred credits. Do I have one hundred credits?"

There were murmurs in the crowd, but the slaver didn't wait for a response. He grabbed the Folta by her face, forcing her mouth open, showing her dark, glistening teeth. "In perfect condition. Never broken. Never lashed. Never disciplined. Sixteenth generation servant. Can clean. Can serve. Can cook. Biologically bred on Nivigian slave farms to work any manor of home or office. Have kids? Then you have a nanny. A built in tutor. Have a pet? She'll tend to them too. Make no mistake this is one of the best servants you will buy in your many centuries in the expanse." He pushed her face away. "But wait. That's not all. She draws. She juggles. She dances. She prances. And, best of all, just wait until you hear her sing!"

Someone in the crowd coughed.

The slaver turned and glared at the Flota. "Well? What in the gods names are you waiting for. I said SING!"

It was unlike anything Kit had ever heard before. High, and fluid, and multi-tonal. She clicked through every note in the spectrum, and even hit some that he'd never heard in his life. A sound that seemed wholly unnatural, yet undeniably beautiful.

It only lasted a few seconds before the slaver clapped his hands and shouted, "One hundred credits! One hundred credits! A steal. The greatest bargain you will find here or in any market in the whole of the Empire. One hundred credits! One hundred credits! Who will give me one hundred credits?"

"One hundred!" someone shouted from behind.

"Two hundred!" came another.

"Two hundred credits? Two hundred credits?" said the slaver with some satisfaction. "Does anyone offer four?"

"Four hundred!" shouted a voice from somewhere behind them.

"Do I hear five?" asked the fat Suul-Manee. "Surely she's worth five! Don't forget, when you purchase through NorthCom free use of our breeding matrix is included in the price! This one will produce many healthy and obedient children. Why, she's not just a servant. She's an investment into the future! Match her. Breed her. Sell her. It's a deal that can't be beat!"

"Five hundred!"

"Six!"

"One thousand!" shouted a nearby Mog.

"Come now," responded the slaver. "Come now. The Folta are bred for obedience. BRED FOR OBEDIENCE! As docile as ursprags as self aware as an old shoe. You will never have a problem with this one and her children even less so. Even two thousand would be a bargain for such a creature!"

"Fifteen hundred!" shouted someone from the back.

The crowd surged. Those from behind pushed toward the platform. Screaming, salivating, throwing ever higher numbers at the fat Suul-Manee. And all the while the slave looked down at her hands. No tears. No fear. Just the blank stare of submission.

Kit and his friends didn't stay to see who won the auction. Bragg managed to find a way through the crowd as another frenzy of bidding erupted and immediately Ash grabbed Kit to follow.

"That is future for all of us," said Bragg matter-of-factly as they managed to climb up to a less crowded street running above the Market.

"No, not all of us," said Ash, her eyes still on the slave auction below. "I'll never let them do that to me." Her expression only hardened, as a dozen different thoughts seem to run through her mind at once. "My world will be free. And if I have to fight you, either of you, I will fight to win."

Bragg shrugged his massive shoulders. "As I say, it is future for all of us. Slave or slaver, matters not."

Kit looked at Ash then at Bragg. His friends. His competition. They were both white team, while he was black. Ash and Bragg might very well face each other in combat, Kit might not end up fighting either one. For that he was grateful. But either way, if one of them won the games, became one of the ascended species, the other two would lose and watch their worlds enslaved.

At least fighters become trainers or gladiators. At least if he lost, he'd never have to endure the auction block. Then Kit thought about his parents, and his little brother, and sadness hit him in his chest and crept up to his throat.

Without a word they each turned away from the Market and the slave auction and continued on into the city. The high street, dark and quiet in comparison to where they'd been, wound around and up away from the center of the city, but like all roads eventually led back at the Boulevard of Battle. Kit for one suddenly wanted to walk all night. Anything to avoid the barracks and the games. Anything to avoid the inevitable.

Eventually they came to a high hill in a quiet residential district. The homes were large half organic monstrosities, glass and grass, bricks and membranes. They stopped on the edge of the furthermost property, the house which resembled more a beached moss covered whale than anything someone would actually live in, and found themselves looking out over the whole of the capital. Half a hundred spires rose into the heavens. Below them the glass dome of the coliseum, and hundreds of glowing, pulsing skyscrapers and smaller buildings jumbled together like the roots of trees. Beyond the city were the mountains and beyond them the outline of distant farm towers, antimatter generators, and the faint straight lines of the space elevators.

Bragg sat himself down in the grass and said, "I think I walk no more."

For a moment none of them said another word. They just watched the flicker of the lights, and the spark and fire of starships entering and leaving the atmosphere. It looked a lot like a meteor shower that Kit had once watched from his backyard in Michigan.

"It's really kind of beautiful," said Ash.

"Very pretty," agreed Bragg.

Kit watched the dancing lights, mindlessly running his finger over the edge of the implant in his head, thinking of the many millions of beings that lived in the city below them. He wondered what they were all doing. How many of them were happy. How many of them were sad. How many of them would be watching the games. How many of them would root for him to win.

Kit thought about his world. He thought about Bolts. He thought about the decisions he'd made since he arrived, and about the decisions that loomed before him.

He could play their game and win. Embrace the terrible violence within him. Become of the ascended. Or he could refuse, like Bolts had. And witness the end of Earth. He still wasn't sure if his world was worth saving but he knew he didn't want to see it destroyed.

The milkwomen believed that the gods set the rolls. Bolts had said that there was truth in that. But what truth?

Kit barely noticed when Ash put her hand on his, squeezing his fingers. He gave her a smile. Maybe she would win? Maybe she should win? Maybe neither of them would get past the first round?

"You know, I was thinking," she began, "that the kind of technological advancement necessary to construct nano as sophisticated as that of the Masters, or even the construction of the World Ship, or even the Motherships in orbit for that matter, does not strictly align with the kind of technology we've seen on the capital. Don't you think it's odd that the Master's home world is not more advanced? Maybe I'm giving them too much credit, but one would think that if they developed nanotech ten thousand years ago, especially nanotech advanced enough to manipulate matter the way that priestess did in the opening ceremony, and given the sort of exponential growth that occurs with such tech progression, I don't think it would be wrong to assume a civilization far more advanced than this one." She paused, considered, frowned, and said, "Of course it is possible that the heavy reliance on slavery has slowed, if not entirely stopped their forward momentum but I wonder if-" She looked at Kit and said, "What is it?"

The smile he had on his face grew wider as he said, "You talk real fast."

She reddened, let out a laugh, and punched him in the arm all in the span of a second. And then they both started laughing.

"What funny?" asked Bragg.

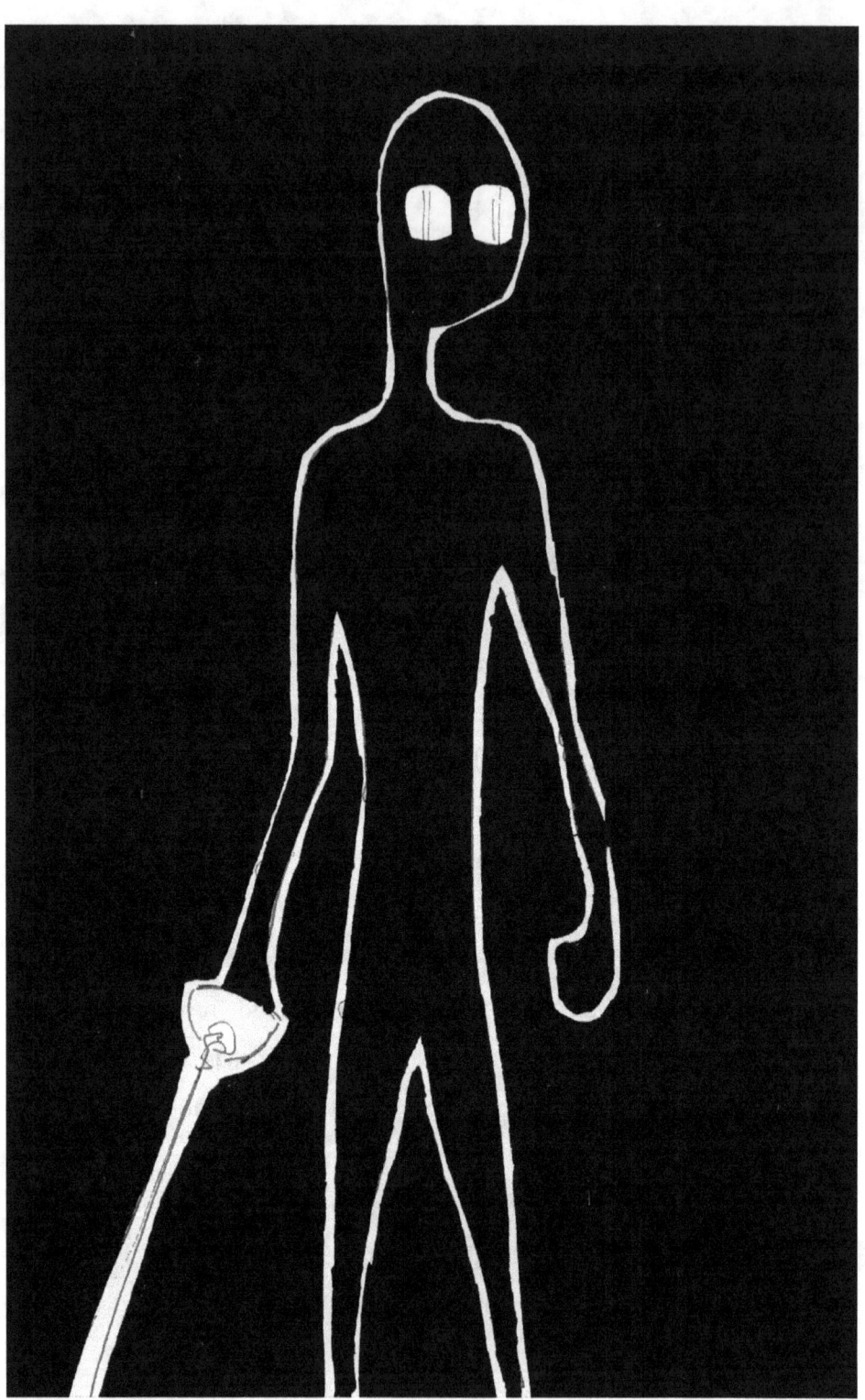

110 **kp dawes**

Chapter 9: The Blight

That night, Kit's dream changed again.

His house in Michigan. Mom and little brother doing a craft project. Dad on the couch reading *The History of the American Slave Trade*, or, *A Century of Genocide: Armenia to Rwanda*, or, *The Crusades: The First Holy War*. A racket outside. Then out the front door. The tools gone. The project complete. A crowd gathered, even larger this time.

The workman: "Come to see what we've built? Then what are you waiting for? Go on. Go on have a look."

And when normally Kit would walk to the scaffold and feel the pain of the electrical discharge as his hand grazed the plastic sheeting, this time he hesitated.

"What are you waiting for?" asked the workman. "Go on."

Kit scanned the crowd and then peeked over his shoulder to his parents and little brother standing on the stoop.

"No," he said. "No, I'm not going to do it."

The workman said, "You have to do it. You have to see what we've built."

Kit shook his head, "No. If I touch it I'll get shocked again."

The workman put his large mitt on Kit's shoulder and said sternly, "Then find another way."

Kit opened his eyes, shot up and clutched his forearm. He was awake. It was morning. The pain was back, like fire, now spread beyond his arm to his shoulder. Muscles constricting. Heart pounding. It was a few minutes before it was gone.

What's happening to me?

He skipped breakfast. He knew he should eat but couldn't, he wasn't hungry. He went straight to the gym and found Bolts already there waiting for him. The trainer was fiddling with a screen, looking over Kit's data for the previous day.

When Kit approached, Bolts switched the screen off and said, "The first round starts today. All sixteen matches, black and white. You are scheduled for this evening. Your opponent is a Blight."

Kit had seen the Blight most every day but never once interacted with him. He was an eel-skinned creature with three sharp fingers on each hand, white on white eyes, and not a hair anywhere on his body. He looked more like a shadow than a living creature.

"He'll be wielding a sword much like yours," continued Bolts. "And has two primary physical advantages: he is extremely flexible, able to bend his body considerably more than any other competitor you might face, and can achieve great height when jumping. In fact, you're most likely to spend much of the time in the arena just trying to catch him. His goal will be to exhaust and disorient you."

"So how do I turn his advantages against him?"

Bolts nodded, "Yes, tell me."

Kit twisted his mouth wryly and said, "I don't chase him. I force him to come to me."

"What else?"

Kit considered and said, "Quick attacks, varied patterns."

"Good, then that's what we'll practice today, after your exercises," said his trainer, as he went back to his data.

Kit lingered.

"Can I ask you something?"

Bolts glanced up at him.

"We never- you said you picked me because I was special," said Kit. "What did you mean?"

Bolts studied Kit's face a moment and said, "Is that what you want to ask me?"

Kit shook his head and said, "I've been having these dreams. Always the same dreams. And then in the arena everything–"

"You want to know if you're becoming like the Masters," said Bolts.

"Am I?"

"You'll never be like them," said his trainer.

"But the dream and the speed and–" Kit swallowed. "I don't feel anything when I hurt people."

Bolts considered this and replied, "If there had ever been any indication that you could do as the Masters do, you wouldn't be here now."

Kit instinctively raised his hand to the small implant protruding from his skull, buried under his hair.

"I picked you because I knew you would win," said Bolts. "Now I suggest you start your routine. Your first fight is tonight." And with that he went back to his screen.

Kit went through his daily set – stretches, running, lifting, gravity training, dueling – then spent an extra hour in a fight simulator, customizing the computer opponent to best simulate what he guessed might be the fighting style of the Blight. At lunch he only picked at his food.

"You must eat," Bragg said with some concern. "You must be strong for battle."

Kit pushed his plate away. "Who are you fighting today?"

Bragg pointed across the room with one of his hands as he continued eating with the other three. "One of the insectoids. I cannot tell them apart. Is that wrong?"

Kit took a quick look around the room. The tension was palpable. Fighters were eating quickly. Talking loudly. Kit noticed that Tau's clique had broken up. The pigmented craftee was sitting alone hurriedly shoveling some kind of porridge into his mouth. When their eyes locked, Tau seethed.

"Who you fight today?"

"Blight," said Kit, turning back.

Bragg nodded as he chewed. "I see him in fight simulator this morning. Quiet. Focused. You should eat."

Kit suddenly remembered his mom at the dinner table constantly reminding him to eat. Urging him on whenever his dad would pause mid lecture. "I'm preparing you for what's out there, you should listen," he'd say.

The sound of Ash dropping her tray down on the table brought Kit back into the present.

"I saw that you were fighting the Blight today," said Ash as she sat. "It'll be a hard fight. From what I understand he has great range and flexibility. The key, I think, is to keep him within range while avoiding his counters, which judging by his physiology, will most likely be very random. He'll likely twist in ways you don't expect."

Kit smirked and said, "Good morning."

Ash flushed, composed and said, "My first match is against one of the B'tids. The taller one. Of course I get a craftee in the first round. Makes perfect sense." She stabbed at what looked like a yellow strawberry on her plate. "Are you both ready? I mean, of course you are. But I mean are you psychologically prepared? Don't let the size and noise of the coliseum sap you. Keep your wits and you'll win."

"I just stab with swords and they lose," said Bragg. "Simple."

"Maybe not that simple," said Ash.

"No," said Bragg. "That simple."

The rest of the day dragged. Anticipation made the hours unbearable. Kit spent more time in the simulator, fighting the composite Blight that he'd nicknamed Frog. From what Egg had taught him, Blight didn't have names. They distinguished one another primarily by scent. So Frog would do for the real version as well.

As the sun began to set, Kit tried to force himself to eat, but nothing seemed the least bit appetizing. He wasn't nervous. Just amped up. Ready to get his first match over with.

With an hour left to go he donned his battle suit. Black with charcoal trim. As he did he again examined the patch, which Bolts had added to the shoulder. Round, white on black, a circle at the center, lines radiating outward. He wondered what it meant. The countries of Earth had flags. Was that what this was?

With sword in one hand and helm in the other, Kit met his trainer at the double doors to the Hall of Champions. Inside the coliseum, Kit knew, combat raged. Ash was going toe to toe against the craftee.

"Remember your training," said Bolts by way of greeting. "Don't let the coliseum affect you. First round matches usually weed out the weakest fighters. Those who can't cope with the competition."

"Will you be watching?" asked Kit.

"I will. I'll be in the stands," responded Bolts. "Remember, the crowd is there for a show. As you fight they may come to know you. Even cheer for you. But they are not your allies."

"I'll try to ignore them."

"You won't be able to," responded Bolts.

Just then the Blight, dressed in a battle suit, sword and helm in his arms, escorted by his trainer, a squat Teft'ian, came up beside them. He did not so much as glance in Kit's direction.

Suddenly the screen above the doors flashed and dinged. An automated voice announced: "Winner, Ashvani Khergostraponi, Adlopo. Combat time: 8 minutes, 3 seconds." And Ash's name advanced to round two on the white side of the bracket.

A couple minutes later the gold doors opened and Ash came out of the Hall of Champions, blood stains on her white battle suit, Phlot, the overseer in his red, pristine armor behind her.

Kit smiled at her. "You did it."

Ash nodded gravely, but said nothing as she made her way past him to her room. Kit watched her go for a moment.

"Fighters ready?" asked Phlot.

Kit and the Blight both nodded.

"Then let's get to it," he said with a spark of enthusiasm.

Bolts put his hand on Kit's shoulder and said, "I'll be in the stands."

Two fighters entered the coliseum by way of the Hall of Champions, but only the winner came back. Kit wasn't sure what happened to the losers, but he knew they did not return to the barracks.

As they made their way down the hall – blue light, column, nook, blue light, column, nook – Kit thought about how unreal it all seemed. How after so many years he was finally there, about to meet the test he'd been training for, and yet nothing about it felt right. He could be anybody, at anytime, in anyplace.

Halfway down the corridor Kit could feel the floor plates vibrating. The clamor rising. Another few meters and the noise grew deafening. The vibration turning to a quake. And when they reached the end, on the other side of the doors, they found blinding light and the fury of three hundred thousand slavers rapt by bloodlust. Screaming twisted faces that all seemed to melt into a wall of color and flesh.

Phlot led them to the midway point of the arena. Equal distance to the white and black start pads. Six gravity wells hummed noisily around them, and above, no less than ten floating platforms, arranged at various heights, rotated in a brilliant clockwise spiral. Above that the screens and glass and stars.

Phlot turned on his heels, Kit and the Blight following suit. In the pavilion, flanked by eight golden Champions, sat Lord Emperor Aejus'lobine and his imperial court. The two fighters and the overseer bowed, Phlot deeply.

"Your grace," shouted the overseer. "I bring you the next two fighters. For your pleasure."

The Lord Emperor glanced in the overseer's general direction and gave him a disinterested nod.

Phlot turned back to Kit and the Blight. "Give them a good show," he said. "I'll see one of you when it's done." And he marched off back toward the set of gold doors through which they entered, his red armor clattering as he walked.

"Fighters, start positions," announced an automated voice.

Kit looked to his opponent, hoping to offer some kind of gesture of fair play, but the Blight was already walking away. *Oh well,* thought Kit.

As he turned toward his start pad the coliseum, raging with noise, seemed to spin around him. Colors looked smeared across his vision. Detail was absent. The stench of metal, blood, and sweat was in everything. He felt weakened by it. Pulled down by it. *I should've eaten*, he thought.

It was overwhelming to be sure, but as he got in position and slipped his helm on his head, he could feel the disorientation slowly ebbing. As the countdown began and the fever of the crowd grew more frenzied, Kit felt his heartbeat slowing. His breathing steadying. His nerves settling down.

...8, 7, 6...

This was it. From here on in every fight counted. Every fight meant the difference between slavery and ascension. Every strike possessing the power to unmake whole civilizations.

...5, 4, 3...

Still and silent, he thought. *Let him come to me. Don't tire yourself. Do not be predictable. Be ready for anything.* His breathing was down to almost nothing. His sword, gripped tightly in his hands, was now a part of his body. This was it. This was it. He was ready.

...2, 1, FIGHT!

He was expecting a slowing. Three quarters speed. Sharp mind, excellent focus. It did come, but what he felt first was an electrical shock surge through his arm and shoulder. Muscles contracting. Pain at a scale of ten. He grit his teeth so hard he thought he might break them. It was all he could do as not to drop his sword right there and then.

He'd felt this pain before, of course. It was the same as in his dream. The same as when he was ripped out from sleeping. Pure white and coursing through his body like blood. And then a heartbeat later came the slowing. A sensation like being pulled out of his body. Hanging just over his head and shoulder. Watching from a great distance. Nothing at stake.

When the initial spike of pain drifted away, Kit glanced at the Blight just in time to see him leap off his start pad, some fifteen meters into the air. He could jump higher and faster than Kit had expected. By the time Kit moved off his own pad, the Blight, like a frog, had already landed on one platform, and leapt across another two. He used his whole body to jump, his legs crunching and snapping like coils.

The crowd was going wild. Screams, jeers, cheers, applause, all faded together into an ear-splitting wall of sound. But for Kit all there was, was the rhythm of his breath and a distant roar like the sound of the ocean in a seashell.

He took his time and eased back to the center of the arena, a few steps from a gravity well. The Blight was still vaulting. Climbing. Another platform. And another. And another. Higher with every stride, hoping to lure Kit into following.

Kit dug in and braced himself, sword raised high. Watching. Waiting. All the while the Blight leaped from platform to platform circling him like a black jaguar stalking its prey.

The Blight were an advanced civilization, Kit knew from Egg, living in vast, crystalline, city-states on a beautiful dark green globe. Although divided amongst clans, the species worked collaboratively to preserve their mutual longevity. The only violence known to the Blight occurred when a member of a clan reached maturity. The newly initiated had to then participate in a ritual hunt and find and slay a creature of their choosing. The more ferocious the creature, the greater the honor and the higher the social position.

Kit wondered if Frog had ever been on the hunt or if this fight now was in his mind some version of it.

Suddenly the Blight leapt again, but this time down, his sword ready, right down on top of Kit. It was by a hair that he managed to avoid the impact.

Kit rolled, backed up, and dug in again just in time for the Blight to strike. Once. Twice. Three times. Each hit blocked. Just barely.

It wasn't Frog's speed so much as his ability to bend and shift his body in such ways that seemed unnatural and were unexpected. He was able to strike from the right, then from the left, up and down, without once taking a step. Even at Kit's level of clarity, even at the dial set to slow, the moves were difficult to anticipate, his opponent hard to read.

Kit took a step back, slashed, recoiled, blocked and countered. If he stayed on the defensive he'd lose, he knew. He had to push in. He had to attack.

The Blight jumped. Up and over. Kit spun to meet him and just barely managed to block a thrust. Then another. He stepped in. He countered. He grazed the Blight's armor. Good. The Blight blocked. The Blight countered. He cut Kit's arm. Blood. Pain. Not good. It was a flesh wound, a few centimeters shy of a winning blow.

Kit stepped back. He needed to regroup. Jump a gravity well and regain the offensive. The Blight was faster. He blocked his path, slashing wildly, twisting out of the way whenever Kit would try and counter. The fight took on a maddening pace. They exchanged four hits in under two seconds. Five. Six.

The distant part of him, the observer watching the fight in slow motion couldn't help but be impressed. The Blight was fighting with everything. He understood what was at stake. And that understanding made him desperate. It made him wild. And that's what also made him weak.

Kit pushed back, swung his sword high. The Blight contorted his body and dodged. Jumped up to a platform, then rebounded back down at Kit. Again he barely got out of the way in time and slipped sideways toward a gravity well just catching the edge of it.

The force pushed him diagonally across the wall, but only about three meters. The Blight jumped and caught him blade to blade. They went back and forth again for what seemed like hours. Time uncoiled millisecond by millisecond.

From somewhere far away Kit watched. He began to get a sense for Frog's timing. He could see a routine. What appeared random wasn't random at all.

Kit stepped back again. The Blight was on him. Slashing. Twisting. Two steps back and he would jump. Blocking. Pushing. One step back, twist. Two steps back, jump. And suddenly Kit saw a potential opening.

He dug in again. The blows came feral. The explosion of steel washed out everything. He blocked. He countered. He blocked. He missed. Another slash. Blood. Pain. Another near loss. Another step back. Block. Counter. Block. Block. Block. Kit took two steps back. The Blight jumped, up and over. Slightly faster than before, but lower too.

Another exchange. Another brutal clash. Kit was all defense. All block. No more risks. *Slow and steady*, he thought. *Wait for the opening.* The Blight swung faster. He slashed at Kit faster. He wanted to finish it. He wanted to win.

Kit took two steps back. The Blight jumped. Kit dove to the metal floor and spun. The Blight twisted midair. Kit twisted with him. The Blight tried to slash at Kit. He tried to hit him mid chest. He missed. The blade went long. He landed. Kit jumped and buried his sword in Frog's neck and cut him stem to stern. Blood exploded. The Blight collapsed in absolute agony.

"Winner, Kopper Io Talos, Earth. Combat time: 9 minutes, 20 seconds," announced the voice over the loudspeakers.

Kit raised himself to his feet and looked at his opponent, writhing on the ground. He had just condemned the Blight to slavery. Their city-states would be dismantled. Their people shipped off to half a thousand different worlds. No Blight would ever go on another hunt ever again. Kit knew he should feel responsible. That he should regret. If not for the fate of the Blight, then at the least for the pain he inflicted on his opponent. Yet he felt nothing at all. And for this he hated himself.

As the doors to the Hall of Champions opened, and Phlot slowly made his way toward the center of the arena, only then did Kit again become aware of the three hundred thousand spectators all around him. They were cheering. They were cheering him. They waved their arms and stomped their feet and screamed. And up on the pavilion, Lord Emperor Aejus'Iobine graced him with a tepid smile.

"Your home world is safe for another day, human," said Phlot, keeping his voice above the clamor. "Now bow so we can get out of here."

Kit bowed toward the imperial court and followed the overseer back out. As they crossed the threshold he glanced over his shoulder. The Blight was being escorted out of the arena by a fat Suul-Manee who looked strangely familiar, via a small door off to the side. Briefly he considered asking Phlot what would become of Frog, but he already knew the answer.

When they emerged back in the barracks Bolts was already waiting for him, standing just behind a craftee in black and a reptilian in white ready to head in for their match.

"Are you alright?" asked Bolts.

Kit glanced down and noticed for the first time that his hand was trembling.

"It's adrenaline," said his trainer. "It will wear off."

Kit swallowed. His head was spinning. "Now what?" he asked.

"Rest," said Bolts. "You did well."

"Did I?"

Once in his room, Kit stripped out his battle suit and helm. He stowed his sword in his locker and stepped into the shower. He set the water to scorching and stood in the spray and the steam, his head resting against the stone of the tile.

He wanted to make himself cry. He wanted to make himself feel. Sadness. Anger. Rage. But nothing would come. He didn't feel anything.

Chapter 10: The Rocknid

In stasis he had asked Egg, "What gives them the right?"

The Al'tkash boy looked at him sidelong and said, "You know, just cause we're in your head doesn't mean I can read your mind."

"What I mean is," responded Kit, "why do the Masters get to decide the fate of all the worlds in the galaxy?"

Egg said: "They're the biggest and the strongest."

"Yeah," said Kit, "but does that mean they have to enslave and murder people?"

"Power corrupts."

"But they can't think that," said Kit, remembering his dad's lectures. "People who do bad things usually believe that what they're doing is right."

"They're not people," said Ash. "They're a very old and highly advanced alien species changed over thousands of years by the technology they control."

"But if we're all the same–"

"We're not all the same," said Egg. "Life is more than just biology, which in itself is diverse, if narrow. It's also psychology, culture, history."

"So they just have games, and slaves, and destroy whole systems because that's the way it is?" Kit shook his head. "There has to be a reason."

Egg considered and said, "Do you recall hearing about the Highborne?"

Kit nodded. Ms. Moffat had mentioned the Highborne on the first day of class. "They were conquered by Aejus'lobine."

"Not conquered," said Egg. "Exterminated."

The walls of the classroom shifted to reveal a massive brown world surrounded by rings.

"The Highborne were a race of quadrupeds from a planet in a highly volatile corner of the galaxy," the walls shifted again to reveal a gargantuan four-legged, two-armed creature with armored violet skin, and an elongated head crowned with ridges, and horns. "They were an advanced species. Not at the level of the Masters, but advanced enough to have started colonizing, even conquering other systems. By the time they were discovered, they had become the dominant power in their sector." The walls shifted a third time, showing a ravaged world, grey with ash and soot. "The Highborne were immortal. They considered themselves gods. They believed that all other life was an insult to their divinity. When the Highborne found an inhabited world, they would wipe life out entirely."

"That sounds familiar."

"No," said Egg. "The Highborne were worse. They didn't enslave other species. They didn't mine other worlds or force their inhabitants to play games for them. They eradicated life. Every microbe. They wanted to be the only life in the universe."

"What happened?" asked Kit.

The wall shifted again to a space battle. Thousands of starships swirled around them, lights flashing, as explosions detonated. Asteroids were fired back and forth like cannon balls had been once hundreds of years ago on Earth. Capital ships banked slowly. Among the vessels were half a dozen motherships and the multi-tiered World Ship, a whole artificial planet rotating under its central dome.

"The war lasted hundreds of years," said Egg. "Many trillions died. At one point, an entire Imperial fleet was destroyed. But in the end, if you believe the official account, Lord Emperor Aejus'lobine was able to turn the tide. The Highborne were destroyed."

"Do you believe the official account?"

Egg shrugged and the walls became walls again, "Nothing is ever as it seems. But the Highborne were bad, very bad, there's no doubting that."

Kit crossed his arms, "How does this give them the right?"

Egg said: "If it wasn't for the Masters, the Highborne, eventually, might have destroyed all life in the galaxy."

"Do you believe that?" asked Kit.

"It doesn't matter what I believe," he responded. "It matters that the Masters believe it. That without their guidance and protection, the universe would be a dark and chaotic place. They see themselves as guardians of life, even if it means exterminating life to protect it. By this logic to serve them is a gift, to ascend is the greatest of honors and responsibilities."

"Do you believe that?" asked Kit again, more forcefully.

Egg paused and said, "There's no way to know how life may have developed across the galaxy if the Masters had not interfered."

"That's not an answer," said Kit.

"Yes it is," said Egg. "Just not the one you wanted."

Egg's words churned in Kit's head all throughout the second day of the games. Through breakfast, morning training, and lunch. It was all he could think about. Which was fine as none of the sixteen remaining fighters, Ash and Bragg especially, seemed very talkative.

Both of his friends had survived the first round, but despite three years of conditioning, neither seemed completely prepared for the games. Truth be told even Kit had underestimated the intensity of his opponent, the difference being that unlike Ash and Bragg he didn't really feel the consequences. It was their first time shedding blood. Even Bragg, who had fought Tau, had never hurt another living being as to kill them. They were shaken by it. Changed. But not Kit. He was still numb.

So he remained quiet all morning and through lunch, and after, thinking. Having spent three years with Bolts he didn't mind the silence.

That evening Kit went back to his room and donned his battle suit and helm. He took his sword out of its locker and took extra time to clean the blade. Hypnotic steel never needed sharpening, but Kit had gotten into the habit of checking its sharpness against the soft tissue of his thumb all the same. He drew a cut and watched it mend just after a single drop of blood managed to escape. It stung for a few heartbeats after.

His opponent was the rocknid. Nearly five meters of solid grey armor, the composition of stone, supported on two tree trunk thick legs and wielding two massive spiked maces. Kit had heard that in the first round the rocknid crushed his reptilian opponent with such force that it took the nano a full half-minute to reassemble his bones. The pain had probably been excruciating.

Just as with the Blight, Kit had not exchanged a word with his opponent, though he'd seen him every day. Now as he stepped onto his start pad, the crowd of the coliseum cheering them lustily, he wished he'd had.

The Soof, the name the rocknids used for themselves, originated on a hostile, volcanic world about one hundred seventy thousand years ago, according to Egg. They were a primitive culture, living in large roving tribes that sustained themselves on hunting the mega beasts that dominated their planet. They didn't have starships. They didn't have advanced technology. But they were intelligent, sentient beings, and according to the Masters were ready to compete in the games.

As the countdown began the roar from the crowd swelled. *This was the fight they've been waiting for all day*, Kit thought. A small pink human against a monster made of rock.

Kit readied himself. He had to stay calm, but knew also that in this fight speed was the key. His opponent was massive, powerful, but slower. Slower to act, even slower to counter. If Kit had any hope it was to stay agile. Use the platforms. Use the gravity wells. Use the–

Suddenly a claxon filled the coliseum and the countdown stopped abruptly. The crowd, cheering just a second earlier was now half laughing half booing. The rocknid had stumbled off his start pad, resetting the countdown and stared, disoriented at the stands and the frenzied spectators. Even from across the arena, Kit could feel the vibrations of the rocknid's steps as he shuffled around.

At that moment the doors to the Hall of Champions burst open and Phlot came storming out, his red armor clattering, a scowl across his meaty face. It had taken the overseer almost ten minutes to get the rocknid through the Hall of Champions. The creature had refused to go at first. Now Phlot had clearly run out of patience.

To the delight of the crowd, the overseer stormed up to the rocknid and pulled a short electrified whip from his belt, screaming at him furiously. It was impossible for Kit to make out what was being said, but it was a strange sight. No matter how imposing the Mog might be he still barely reached the rocknid's waist. Now he stood under him lobbing threats and threatening gestures as though talking down to a child. Whatever was said seemed to work as after a few moments the rocknid hesitantly stepped back onto the start pad.

Phlot lingered for another few moments. More screaming. More wild gestures. Only when he seemed absolutely certain that he got his point across did he leave the arena. The countdown restarted a second later.

Kit didn't know what he was feeling. Was it sympathy? Was it pity? Something in the way Phlot yelled at the rocknid didn't sit right. It seemed too familiar. At home. At school. He remembered how that felt. It didn't feel good.

The claxon sounded again. The countdown stopped again. The rocknid had stepped off the pad again. This time no one laughed. The entire stadium was booing. Some of the spectators were throwing whatever they had at hand onto the arena floor. Food mainly.

The doors to the Hall of Champions flew open again. Phlot stormed out, even angrier than before, the whip already in his hand. He crossed the distance to the rocknid and without a word started flogging him. Four quick strikes. Another four after. The rocknid let out a wail of pain and fell to the floor on one gigantic knee. The creature's armored skin was too thick for the whip to penetrate. It was the electrical shock he was reacting to.

Phlot struck him three more times then started screaming again. He was pointing wildly at Kit. Again the thunder of the crowd made it impossible to hear, but to Kit it seemed pretty obvious. *Kill him! Kill him and you can leave!*

The rocknid got back to his feet, his eyes on Kit. Phlot told him something else. Again he pointed at Kit. Then back to the rocknid. More screams. Threats. Then Phlot stormed back out, the doors shutting behind him.

The countdown began again. Kit raised his sword. The rocknid was staring at him. Two small black eyes in a massive craggily face. He was holding his spiked maces tightly and he was shaking from head to toe. *He's terrified,* Kit realized.

...8, 7, 6...

Fighting a scared opponent could be more dangerous than fighting a skilled opponent, Kit knew from his training. Fear amped aggression and unpredictability. Fear made a fighter wild.

...5, 4, 3...

Kit quickly surveyed the arena. There were only four gravity wells, one at each point, but five extra platforms. The platforms were arranged in three tiers, the first and third moving clockwise, the middle tier moving counterclockwise. In the center two platforms rose up and down like elevators. *Move quickly*, he thought. *Move out of reach.*

...2, 1, FIGHT!

Electrical surge across Kit's arm and shoulder. Muscles contracting. Pain. At least this time Kit had known to expect it. And on the other side the world in slow motion. Even slower than before. Half speed at best. Maybe less. The rest of the coliseum slipped away. The Masters, the ascended, the Imperial court and the Champions all went imperceptible. There was only David and Goliath.

He shook off the discomfort and dashed for the nearest gravity well. At the corner of his eye he could already see the rocknid charging at him. A mountain of stone descending on him, massive maces of spikes glistening against the bright lights of the arena. He roared, the sound stretched into a rumble, his fear turned to blind rage. As the rocknid ran, the floor shook violently.

Kit jumped on the gravity well and was thrown horizontally against the wall, a quarter turn around the battlefield. As the rocknid turned after him, in slow motion looking like an avalanche, swinging wildly after him, Kit jumped to the next gravity well and again made a second quarter turn against the wall. The rocknid spun, roaring.

Keep moving, keep him disoriented, Kit thought as he jumped for the next gravity well.

By this point the rocknid knew where he was going and lunged for the third gravity well, hoping to crush Kit on the pad. Luckily, even at full speed the creature was so big and bulky that it was impossible not to predict his next move. At the last minute Kit shifted direction, took a running jump and slashed the rocknid across the side, just under its right arm. The creature suddenly turned, screaming, and sent one of the maces straight down on Kit, the latter just barely scrambling out of the way in time.

It took Kit a second to realize the fight hadn't ended. That the cut he'd made wasn't enough to end the match. The rocknid's armor was too thick. He was too big. *This is going to be harder than I thought.*

Kit raced away from the rocknid, trying to put as much distance between them as he could, but his opponent closed the distance in half the time. One mace came down to Kit's right, another to Kit's left. Each impact left a crater in the arena floor. Every hit shook the ground beneath him.

He shifted direction. Dodged and shifted again. Dodged again. Slid two meters and tried to hack off the rocknid's leg at the ankle. Nothing.

Kit just barely reached a gravity well. A quarter turn around the arena. For a split second the rocknid lost him. It was enough. Kit raced for the center and jumped on one of the elevators. From there he jumped to the first tier of platforms. The rocknid saw him. He swung one of his maces up at him. Kit jumped just as the platform exploded into splinters and fire.

Need to get higher, thought Kit as he bounded across two more platforms. The rocknid came again. He swung. He missed. Barely.

Kit jumped. Jumped again. The second tier was too high. The vertical platforms were both, for the moment, out of reach.

Another platform exploded. Kit jumped. Was about to jump again, but stopped suddenly. There was a gap where the first platform had been. He had to jump down or double back. This time he wasn't fast enough.

There, in slow motion, he watched the creature's mace come at him. Even as he moved he knew it was too late. One of the hypnotic steel spikes tore at his chest and down his abdomen. His battle suit tore. Blood splattered. And

Kit fell as the platform disintegrated under him. Sparks. Flames. A blast of carbon polymer.

He landed hard on his side as platform fragments rained down on top of him. He grabbed at his mended chest. *Is this how it ends?* The rocknid took a step back. He was looking up. He didn't see him. And Kit realized there was no flash. No victory announcement. Maybe another centimeter and it would've been over, but somehow he was still in it.

The rocknid took two more steps back, noticed Kit down on the floor and raised his maces to strike. Kit rolled out of the way as they came down. Rolled again at the impact. He was missing his sword. *Where is it? There! Fifteen meters away.*

As the rocknid tore his maces out of the bowls of two fresh craters, Kit jumped to his feet and ran for his sword. The rocknid swung a mace after him. Kit slid, clearing the hypnotic spikes by a millimeter. Out of the slide into a sprint he grabbed his blade by the grip. He turned. The rocknid swung again. Another perfect dodge. Another near miss.

Kit stole a glance at the platforms. Five remaining on the first tier. Six on the second. Four on the third, narrowing like a Christmas tree. If he could reach the top he might have a chance.

The rocknid came at him again. His swings were coming harder. Wilder. Faster. There was no way to block him. No way to deflect. If the rocknid made contact again the fight would be over for good.

Kit dodged. Kit sprung. Kit darted. Kit became an evasion expert. Craters formed around him. Bowls. Holes. Metal shards rose high into the air and made breathing difficult. He pushed toward the vertical platforms. The timing had to be right. The timing had to be perfect. Another near miss. Another. Another. All Kit could see was the glint of steel. All Kit could hear was the beat of his heart.

Kit pushed in. Kit got in close. He tried to stay under his swings. *Stay on his heels. Keep him turning.* He swung his sword as he could. He cut the rocknid across the back. Across both legs. He tore into his knee caps. Nothing, no effect except to make the giant angrier.

The rocknid roared frustrated and raised his arms for a heavy blow. Kit saw his opening. Kit ran straight for the rocknid just as the maces came down. He bent his knees. He raised his sword. He slid free of the maces between the rocknid's legs. He swung and cut at his heels. He cut at where his Achilles tendons should be.

The rocknid shrieked. He lost his footing and dropped as Kit rose and ran toward the vertical platforms. He didn't dare turn to look over his shoulder. One of the elevators touched down and immediately started up again. He pushed himself harder. Ten meters. Nine meters. Eight meters. The platform climbed. Higher. Higher. Six meters. Five meters. Four meters. He knew the rocknid was probably already up. He could feel the vibration in the floor plates. He could sense him coming. Two meters. One meter. He leapt and caught it with his free hand.

As he cleared the first tier, Kit pulled himself up. A mace swing came after him. Another platform exploded. He got to his feet as he cleared the second tier. He looked down to see the rocknid begin tearing at the remaining first tier platforms and swinging at the second.

When he got to the top, Kit stepped off. From the third tier he could take in the whole coliseum. The crowd was stomping and cheering. In the pavilion several members of the Imperial court were on their feet.

Kit looked down. A mace came flying up at him. He leapt. Two platforms exploded up on the third tier. Another platform exploded down on the second.

Kit looked down. The rocknid was roaring. Kit took a long breath. He'd only get one chance at this and if he failed he'd lose. He'd lose painfully. The rocknid would grab him and crush him and stomp him so hard there might not be anything left.

Kit looked down. The rocknid was climbing. He put one massive foot on a first tier platform and raised himself up with his free hand, reaching for the second. There weren't many platforms left and since the two levels were moving in opposite directions he was having a hard time moving any higher.

Kit bent his knees and readied himself. He waited for his platform to come around. Waited for his opponent to get to the second tier. *Slow and steady*, he thought. *Have to be perfect. Have to time it right.*

The rocknid grabbed onto a second tier platform, letting his legs fly free and at the same moment Kit jumped. Up and down and right onto the rocknid's back, plunging his hypnotic blade down through the creature's neck. Tearing through his armor and flesh underneath, driving toward his chest.

A shudder went through the giant as though an earthquake and immediately he lost his grip on the platform. Suddenly they were both falling and Kit pushed off, pulling his sword out clean. He hit the floor and rolled as the rocknid collapsed behind him like a meteorite, crushing more floor plates as he landed.

The lights flashed. "Winner, Kopper Io Talos, Earth. Combat time: 10 minutes, 41 seconds," announced the voice over the loudspeakers, just barely audible over the roar of the coliseum.

Kit stopped. He raised himself. He glanced at his blade. It was soiled pitch black. He surveyed the arena. It looked like a war zone. He took off his helmet. The crowd was going wild. Kit couldn't help but smile. Then he stopped himself and grimaced. He looked over at the rocknid, still flat on his back, moaning softly. He finally felt something and the realization scared him.

He felt satisfaction.

136 **kp dawes**

Chapter 11: The Optwap

All competition was postponed the next day. The damage to the arena was extensive following Kit's battle against the rocknid and would require nearly 20 hours to complete. No one seemed to mind. Not the remaining eight fighters who welcomed a day of rest before the start of the third round and not apparently the Masters, who according to Phlot, were very happy with what was being described as the most thrilling night of combat in nearly a thousand years.

The barracks felt very empty. In two short days twenty-four fighters had been eliminated from the games, two by Kit's own hand, their worlds lost to slavery.

Ash and Bragg were still in the fight, as was Tau, the last remaining craftee. The others included an insectoid called Brisk. A Tobrus from the planet Tobra, whose most defining characteristic was his lack of skin. A short, rotund, but powerful dwarf-like creature called an Uusk. And Kit's next opponent, the tall, lean, bear-like Optwap.

"Just think," said Ash as they sparred in one of the training rooms after their morning routines, "if you win you might end up fighting Tau again."

"Is Tau still the favorite to win?" asked Kit, blocking one of her knives with his sword.

"After your last fight I'm not so sure," she replied with a smirk. "I heard the odds makers are split, though I'm still in the running."

Kit didn't know what to think at the prospect of fighting Tau a second time. They hadn't exchanged a word since their first and only fight in the practice arena, an occasional glare from the craftee their one lasting form of communication. Tau was a hard fighter and only failed to finish him because he relied too heavily on his greatest physical advantage. It had made him sloppy in the arena and Kit had no doubt that he'd be more disciplined if they ever faced each other again.

"How did you know to cut the rocknid through the back of his neck?" asked Ash as she thrust a knife at him. "Did you research his species' vulnerabilities? I wasn't able to find much myself. Apparently their dermal layers are nearly impenetrable."

"I didn't," Kit responded, blocking again. "I just picked what I thought might be the softest target."

She laughed as she dodged his counter, "Not everyone has the same anatomy. Although curiously many species share the same basic structure, the variances are often great enough that it's best not to assume. Still, the similarities are astounding. It does lend credence to the Unification Theory, as well as the core dogma of several hundred religions. One creator for all the universe. All beings made in that great being's image. I'm sure humans have a similar belief system, or at least did at one point in your history. My people were never much for religion, at least not that we would classify it as such. But my point is, you were lucky."

"It worked," said Kit with a shrug.

Kit thought about the rocknid. About him writhing on the broken arena floor. He thought about the satisfaction he felt at the sight of him. He shuddered.

"What do you think happens to them?" he asked, as Ash pushed in with her knives, forcing him back.

"Who?"

"The fighters," said Kit. "The ones that lose."

"One of us will find out soon enough," she responded. "And by that I mean–"

"I know what you mean," he said.

Ash lashed at his head. He blocked and countered, swinging his blade at her chest. She fell back.

"I heard that they're taken to another section of the coliseum," she said, blocking his attack. "Somewhere below the arena. Perhaps right under the arena floor? I heard they stay there until they can be processed."

"Processed?" he asked, as Ash managed to push him away.

"Not all fighters become gladiators," she said launching one of her throwing knives. "Some aren't entertaining enough." She smirked as he deflected the blade. "Nothing you need to worry about. I'm sure when you lose to me you'll become a trainer or a prize fighter. Apparently there's wealth to be made in the touring circuits."

Kit raised his hand to signal a break. "What happens to the ones who don't become gladiators?"

Ash walked to a table against the near wall and retrieved a bottle of water, sweat glistened against her bare head "I don't know. I think they just get enslaved with the rest of their species. I would assume anyway. Though honestly I'm not sure what logical sense it makes to keep fighters around in any capacity."

"Why's that?"

Ash shrugged as she swallowed down a slug of water, and said: "What benefit is there for a slave society to keep a stable of trained fighters? Especially ones with a grudge. It would seem to me that you would be inviting insurrection."

"Has there ever been a slave revolt?"

Ash took down another slug and said, "Not that I know of, but on a long enough timeline it's bound to happen sooner or later."

Kit wiped his brow with a towel and considered for a moment the kind of slaves that humans might make.

"Do you think your people would resist the Masters?" asked Kit.

Ash took a longer drink from her bottle and said, "My people will never be slaves."

"If you lose—"

"No," she said firmly. "My people will not be slaves. I've seen it."

Kit frowned at her. "What do you mean that you've *seen* it?"

Ash placed her water bottle back on the table and said, "I told you that my people study genetic memory. Look beneath the essence of all that a person was to their core. Emotion. Reason. Dreams. In the dream state the mind is free to roam and so the individual can glimpse fragments of all time. All that was, all that is, all that will be. Pieces of the space-time constant. But only pieces. Small, often incomprehensible." She paused, considered, and continued. "A few hundred years ago we discovered something remarkable. An individual only spies fragments, but the group sees wholes, and the larger the group the clearer the picture. Collective genetic memory thus allows for a true understanding of what may come."

Kit shook his head, "So you're saying that through this collective memory you've seen the future?"

Ash nodded.

"What did you see?" he asked.

Ash locked her jaw, considered again, and finally said, "Struggle. Death. But ultimate victory."

"But you said your people wouldn't resist the Masters," said Kit.

"No, I said my people would never be enslaved," corrected Ash.

Kit crossed his arms, "Your people will fight and your people will win."

Ash smirked, "Perhaps we won't fight alone."

Kit thought about his dream.

"So why bother to compete if the future is written?" he asked.

Ash went blank and after a moment replied, "There is always a choice. To fight or not to fight. To act or not to act. To rise or fall. One choice can mean everything. When the time comes the right choice must be made."

"That makes no sense," said Kit. "If the future is written and everything is decided then there is no choice."

Ash smirked, "You're assuming again."

Kit sighed. "I liked you better when you did the talking for both of us."

Ash flushed and hit him in the arm.

Later that afternoon as Kit sat in his room, eyes closed, legs crossed, trying to meditate the way Bolts had taught him what now seemed like a lifetime ago, his mind kept wandering. To the rocknid, to the Blight, to his dream, and to his dad. Especially to his dad.

He remembered a time in the summer just a few weeks before he was taken, when his parents were fighting as they often did, and his dad decided to pack up the car and take him on a trip out west. Just the two of them. A cooler in the back and endless road.

The plan had been to drive to the Rocky Mountains, but they only reached as far as the Black Hills of South Dakota, his dad marking off landmarks as though the whole thing was some kind of shopping trip. Badlands. Check. Mount Rushmore. Check. Crazy Horse. Check. Deadwood. Check. They'd never linger in any one place, just stay long enough to snap a few photos as though to have proof of the their accomplishment. Mainly they'd drive with the radio off, his dad telling him about their country and about their world and how broken it was. A repair project for which no one had the tools.

But Kit also remembered that for hours on end there had been only silence. Nothing beyond the pitch and thud of the tires against the sun-bleached road.

"This is still the original concrete," his dad had told him, "going back to when Eisenhower built the entire highway system."

Kit had hated that trip. He'd been grateful that it only lasted a few days. Glad to be back with his mom and little brother. Glad to be sleeping in his own bed and not in some creepy motel out in the middle of nowhere.

He didn't know why his dad had insisted on it. Why he'd insisted on bringing him along. Kit remembered glancing over at him in the car. Glasses on his face. Eyes lost in the road. Sometimes at night he'd wake to find his dad sitting in the dark at the motel window. Watching the headlights of the trucks flashing past.

Kit remembered his dad smiling many times, but not once did he remember him happy. Like there was perpetually a cloud over him. As though he lived forever in shadow. Other dads weren't like that. Kit hated him for it.

"Eventually all sons must rise beyond their fathers," Bolts had told him once, as though sensing his preoccupation. "On my world it was something we struggled with all of our lives, even long after our fathers had died."

Kit wondered if he'd ever see his dad again, or if he'd spend the rest of his life talking about the Earth that was. Talking about his people the way Bolts spoke of his. Past, buried, long dead. Anecdotes to pass on to some future student from another doomed world. And so on, and so on.

The more time went on the less Kit remembered of Earth. If he lost the tournament eventually it would all be gone. Lingering only in slave songs and a few precious artifacts smuggled out in pockets and secret compartments. All that was the human race reduced to a few coins, jewels, stones. A whole world become little more than the things carried off by its inhabitants.

That night Kit barely slept and for the first time in three years he didn't dream. When his alarm rang he dragged himself out of his cot and stuck his head under the tap. He didn't feel good. He was sore. Awkward. He felt slower somehow.

"Where are you?" asked Bolts at their morning training.

"I'm here," Kit responded.

Bolts stared at him for a moment and said, "No you're not. Where are you?"

Kit flashed red. "I'm right here," he said.

Bolts: "Where are you?"

"Here."

"Where are you? Where are you? Where are you?"

"What do you want me to say?" snapped Kit, frustrated.

"If you don't focus you'll lose."

Kit locked his jaw.

"So I'll ask again," said Bolts. "Where are you?"

"I'm on some stupid alien world far from home fighting for," he shook his head. "I don't even know what I'm fighting for!"

Bolts cocked his head. "You don't know what you're fighting for?"

Kit scoffed. "If I lose, I lose. If I win, I still lose." He wanted to kick something. He wanted to pick something up and hurl it across the room. "I never asked for this! I never wanted to do it! I don't want to be here. I don't want to be here!"

"What's happened?"

Kit balled his hands into fists but then just as quickly relaxed. The truth was that he couldn't answer because he didn't know.

Bolts seemed to consider something and then said, "You *are* here. Accept it or lose." He picked his screen up from off his table, and started tapping commands. "No more training. You can make your choices in the arena tonight."

The anger he had felt just seconds ago vanished, suddenly replaced by anguish. He wanted to try and explain himself. He wanted to try and make sense of what he was feeling. But he had no words to describe it, just the lingering memory of his dad, sitting in the dark at a motel window, watching the headlights of the trucks flashing past.

Kit spent the rest of the day in the fight simulator avoiding any real contact, but that brought little relief. For the first time in months he found it impossible to beat the computer above the intermediate setting. Every opponent seemed faster and stronger, even those he'd beaten a hundred times before. The Mog proved especially difficult, his attacks coming so fast and so brutal that Kit could barely counter before the match was over.

"You human are very sensitive," said Bragg as he and Kit waited for their matches to begin that evening. "Little things bother you very much."

Kit frowned at him, "How many humans do you know?"

Bragg grinned in response.

They were sitting on the second tier of the dorm, staring down at the practice arena, their feet dangling over the side. Kit's fight against the Optwap was first that night. Judging by the swarm of shuttle activity visible through the glass dome above them, the spectators had already begun to file in.

"So will you tell me what is wrong?" asked Bragg. "Or is Hapf burning once again?"

Kit didn't quite understand Bragg's metaphor, so said simply, "I'm just feeling off today."

Bragg nodded knowingly and said, "Not many fighters left. Stakes are high."

"It's not that," said Kit. "I'm not really sure what it is. I couldn't sleep last night."

"Who can sleep?" Bragg said, raising three out of four hands. "I have no sleep in three years."

Kit glanced down at the arena and at the doors leading to the Hall of Champions. "I really liked beating the rocknid. I think I enjoyed beating the Blight too."

Bragg smiled, "They were great victories my friend."

"No," said Kit. "No, you don't understand. I don't like that I liked it."

Bragg gave him a long look and finally said, "You are right. I do not understand."

Kit shook his head and looked back to the arena.

"There is nothing wrong with savoring your victory," said Bragg. "Games are made—"

"But this isn't a game," said Kit, then added under his breath: "I don't want to do this anymore."

For several seconds they sat in silence.

"Did you ever hear of The Temple?" asked Bragg at last.

Kit shook his head no.

"No matter what you may think on it, The Temple is not a building," he paused as though for dramatic effect. "The Temple is a planet. The First World, they call it."

"I never heard of it," said Kit.

Bragg shrugged his large shoulders – all of them – and said, "Not many know of The Temple outside of the Masters. You have Al'tkash trainer besides. How should you ever hear of anything?"

Kit had to concede the point.

"So what about this *Temple*?"

"*The* Temple," corrected Bragg. "It is said to be a planet on which the gods of the Masters live. At the center of the galaxy."

"Aren't there black holes in the center of the galaxy?"

"Makes no matter," said Bragg. "That is where it is."

Kit frowned as Bragg continued, "They say it is the place where all life began. The oldest place. They say that before the Masters, it was the homeworld of another older people. The oldest people. A people who could move whole systems and spin galaxies."

Kit raised a brow. "And you believe it?"

Bragg thought about the question and said, "I don't know, but it is good story, no?"

"But what does it have to do with anything?" he asked. "What does it have with the games?"

"Perhaps nothing," said Bragg, glancing up at the sky beyond the dome. "I fight for my people. For my world. But for me, if I win, I go to this place. I stand on it and take handful of soil in my hand."

"Why?" asked Kit.

"To understand," replied Bragg. "Not only this. But everything."

"From dirt?"

"From dirt," Bragg agreed.

"And if the gods do live there?"

"All the better. Then maybe they can tell me themselves!" said Bragg, laughing. "But my point," he said lifting a finger on one of his hands, "is that you must find your own reasons to fight. A whole world... it weighs too much."

For just a moment, Kit flashed once again to his dad.

***

It all went wrong right from the start. After the countdown ended and the fight began, Kit didn't feel the calm of previous encounters. As the Optwap, a mangle of muscle, fur, claws, and teeth came racing at him from off its start pad, Kit felt something entirely new: terror. Blind terror. His first instinct was to drop his sword and run, but somehow, through sheer will, he held his blade and forced himself to move toward his opponent.

The Optwap were what the Masters called a semi-sentient species. Although they were probably still hundreds of thousands of years from developing anything resembling civilization, or language for that matter, they were capable of reason. Ruled by more than just base instinct. That being said, the story was that this particular Optwap tried to mangle his instructor for weeks before finally accepting the training. Rumor had it that the Optwap were not being seriously considered for ascension, but rather brought in to compete strictly to add entertainment value.

Thanks to Egg, Kit knew better, perhaps not about the Masters' intentions, but certainly about his opponent. He knew for instance that although the Optwap were seemingly ferocious, they were in fact a very passive species, more scavengers than hunters, who dwelled in complex social groups in vast underground cities on a giant planet dominated by animals far more dangerous than them. They didn't dream of dominating their planet or colonizing space, but to put it as Egg had put it, "not all being aspire to the same things."

"But be careful," Egg had warned him. "When cornered, an Optwap can be one of the most dangerous opponents you'll face."

In the time it took Kit to cross two meters, the Optwap had leapt across half the arena floor. In the time it took him to raise his sword to swing, the Optwap was already on him, teeth snapping, claws moving so fast that they seemed to blur. The impact sent them both flying, and as they tumbled, Kit could feel a series of sharp jolts across his arms and midsection. As they rolled his bear-like opponent snapping at his neck, Kit glimpsed a streak of blood across the metal tile, and realized, a little slowly, that it was his.

Kit screamed, in shock and anger and managed to get his feet under the Optwap's chest to push him off. The creature fell hard and instantly rebounded, like a coiled spring. It jumped and was on him again. Its hot breath on Kit's face, teeth glistening. Kit managed to kick it off a second time, but this time didn't hesitate to move.

He was aware that his battle suit was torn in places from the Optwap's sharp claws. He was also aware of the pain he felt across his arms and chest. But the battle was still going. He had to keep going.

Kit didn't know where his sword was but for the moment it didn't matter. With the Optwap on his heels, with the crowd roaring all around them, Kit jumped onto a nearby gravity well. Which, to both his and his opponent's surprise, sent him flying right back into the Optwap like a cannon ball, sending them both sliding in opposite direction.

He took a quick survey of his surroundings. Only two gravity wells on opposite sides of the arena. Only four platforms. One pair spinning clockwise, the other spinning counter-clockwise. It wasn't much to work with. And his sword? With the Optwap already charging at him, still too far away to matter.

Kit decided that the only way he had a chance was to do the unexpected. And despite all of his instincts to run away from the Optwap he decided instead to run toward him. Heart racing, nerves breaking down by the second, Kit raced at his opponent trying to pick up speed along the way. He saw it in his head: as the Optwap leapt up at him, claws slashing to meet his eyes, and nose, and mouth, he'd slide under and away, bank toward his sword.

It didn't work. The Optwap either anticipated Kit's move or else reacted instantly to it. Kit felt more than saw his opponent's claws rip through his left arm, sending waves of pain rushing across his entire body. Blood gushed. Blood splattered. But no sound would leave his throat. He instead went spinning, like a rag doll, landing hard on the metal floor.

No claxon. No end. It hadn't been a killing blow, although his arm felt like it had been severed from his body.

Kit's adrenaline was spiking. Heat release and shivers across all his extremities. But no time. No time. The Optwap was on him again. More blood. More pain. Kit pushed against the creature and felt his muscles snapping. Hot breath and saliva. Razor sharp teeth trying to sink themselves into his neck and face. He pushed. He kicked. He screamed. So loud everyone in the arena fell silent for just a second.

A well-placed kick got the Optwap to recoil. Kit, bloody and sore, shuffled back on his hands, looking desperately for his weapon. Any weapon. Somewhere deep down he could hear Bolts. He was saying something about remaining steady. Something about staying calm. But the words didn't make sense somehow. They were vague and out of context.

Kit regained his footing and dashed for one of the platforms, making it just at the Optwap slashed a gash through his calf. Somehow he held on. Somehow he pulled himself up. By the time he stood the nanos had done their work, but a tremor shot through him all the same. He jumped to the next platform. The Optwap was right behind him. He made the next jump. His timing was off, but he managed to grab hold, barely. The Optwap was right behind him. Kit rolled off the platform. He could see his sword a dozen meters out. Ten. Eight. Six. Four. He lunged, but the Optwap was right behind him.

Before the Optwap pounced, Kit managed to turn his body. As they made contact, Kit managed to grab its claws. And as they collapsed back onto the arena floor, Kit managed to keep it just out of bite range. But it wasn't enough.

They fought for what seemed a long time. Viciously. Desperately. Blindly. Flashes of limbs and teeth and blood. Pain and adrenaline. Spiking. Waning. Kit tried to reach for his sword. Failed. Tried again. Failed again.

"There were these kids at my school who used to pick on me," Kit had told Egg in stasis. "My dad used to tell me never to fight them. To just let them do what they wanted and never fight back."

"Because you could lose?" asked Egg.

Kit shook his head, "Because I could win."

His dad was a harsh man, always telling him and his little brother about how terrible the world was. How terrible people were.

"Even you," his dad had told him. "We all have monsters inside us."

Did Earth deserve to be saved? Did he? He'd felt satisfaction at beating the rocknid. Was he becoming the monster his dad had warned him about?

Just as Kit's defense finally failed him he grabbed his sword. In the same instant that he felt the Optwap's teeth sink into his flesh, he stuck the blade in the creature's side. It wasn't enough. As the pain ripped through him he flashed back again to his dad sitting in the window of that motel. As he felt the bones of his rib cage splinter, he remembered the look in his dad's eyes as he stared out into the darkness of the night. As fear gave way to acceptance, he realized that what he'd seen in his dad was sadness. Deep, profound sadness.

And as the lights of the arena faded and the world closed up around him, he remembered something else from that night on the road, as he hovered between sleep and waking. He remembered his dad sitting next to him stroking his hair. He remembered his dad kissing him on the cheek. He remembered his dad telling him how much he loved him.

"No matter what," he'd whispered to him, "I'll always be proud of you."

Chapter 12: Defeat

For a brief moment Kit thought he was back in Michigan, back in his own bed never having left. But it was only the fleeting deception of waking. As the world flooded back to him the falsity brought tears to his eyes. He caught his breath as to keep himself from crying, but the pain in his heart made his entire chest throb with anguish. For a while he let himself feel the sorrow, if not the tears.

As his conscious mind reset, he began to remember other things too. For one that he'd been defeated by the Optwap. He didn't remember much of it, but he knew at least that he'd lost. He'd lost the game and Earth along with it. Every man, woman, and child doomed to serve the Masters. His father, mother, and little brother. Gone all gone. And yet despite the anguish, he couldn't help but feel a profound sense of relief. As though he was free for the first time. That realization brought on guilt.

He felt the pain again. He felt the tightness in his chest. He wanted to be free. He was glad to be free. But he knew too that he hadn't wanted to be free like this.

Suddenly he couldn't catch his breath. Suddenly he felt the room spinning. He was shaking.

Darkness consumed him. The sorrow returned. Flashes of the arena. Flashes of his dad. They had all taken from him. He gave and they had taken.

Everyone in his life. His parents. His little brother. The kids at school. Even Bolts. They took his happiness. They took his courage. They took him away from home. He was glad to be rid of them all. So why did he feel so miserable?

He remembered his last thoughts as the Optwap ripped into his chest. His dad stroking his hair. His dad telling him how proud he was. It wasn't enough. It would never be enough. But it was all he had, and that made him hurt even more.

Human beings were violent, he reminded himself. They were murderers and destroyers. Slavers and conquerors. Human history was just one atrocity on top of another, leading to what? The destruction of Earth? Maybe the Masters were the only hope there was. Maybe by putting humanity in chains they'd save it. But the thought brought no relief. Just more pain.

It was several minutes before Kit was able to calm himself. Several minutes before he felt strong enough to raise himself up.

He took several long breaths and let his nerves settle. A few more deep breaths and he was able to focus. He was on a bed, surrounded by monitors and strange machines, in an unfamiliar, dark room with a tiny bathroom off to one side. The walls were not unlike those of the barracks, but somehow he instinctively knew he was no longer in the barracks. Only winners were allowed back through the Hall of Champions. He no longer qualified.

As he sat up, Kit realized that the pain in his chest wasn't purely emotional. Beneath his jumpsuit much of his body, but especially his chest, felt raw. For a second Kit wondered how much of his body had been rebuilt by the nano.

"You were asleep a long time," came a voice from the shadows.

Kit jumped slightly. Then after a moment, he noticed a shape stir in the corner.

"Who's there?" asked Kit.

"I apologize, I did not mean to startle you," came the voice again. It was a soft voice.

"Who are you?" asked Kit.

The figure stirred again and slowly came out into the light.

"You," said Kit, frowning. "I didn't know you could speak."

The Blight blinked his large white on white eyes at him. "I learn," he replied.

Kit raised himself up on his elbow, wincing slightly at the discomfort he felt at every movement.

"The pain will go away," said the Blight, the motion of his small mouth barely detectable. "You sustained much damage."

"I remember some of it," said Kit. "Where are we?"

"Under the coliseum," responded the Blight, moving a step closer. "Here the doors are guarded."

Kit understood.

"We wait here until they decide what is be done with us," said the Blight. "Some will go to Gladiator School. Others not so lucky." He looked Kit in the eyes. "You have two points for your two victories. I have zero."

Kit couldn't help but feel guilt.

"Your trainer, the tall one with the spikes in his head, he's been here many times to look in on you," added the Blight. "He seemed... worried."

Kit sat up, and was instantly rewarded by a sharp pain in his head. He reached up and felt the metal edge of the implant under his hair with the tip of a finger.

"How long have I been asleep?" he asked.

"Almost a full day," said the Blight. "The Optwap who defeated you will fight the craftee in just a few hours."

Tau was still in the competition. That wasn't much of a surprise.

"What about white?"

The Blight hesitated a moment and then replied, "Your friends. The grey-skinned girl and the boy with the four arms. They fight each other later tonight." He lowered his head. "I'm sorry."

Kit had always known that it was possible, even likely that he might end up fighting one of his friends in the arena. Somehow he never imagined that they would have to face each other.

"It's terrible what they make us do," said the Blight.

Kit glanced over at the instruments and readouts flanking his bed. He thought about his friends fighting. About Ash's fierce determination. About Bragg's confidence. Neither of them would give an inch. They'd fight to the bitter end. They'd have to.

"What happens now?" asked Kit.

"We wait," replied the Blight. "After the final round the Masters will determine our futures." He paused. "I hope to see my home one last time. Do you think they will let us return home?"

Kit said, "I'm not sure we have homes to go back to."

The Blight seemed to consider his words, and for a little while there was only silence.

"Why are you here?" asked Kit. "Why are you in this room?"

"You defeated me," said the Blight, as though the answer were obvious.

Kit frowned. "So?"

"I wanted to thank you," was the response.

Kit was taken aback. "You want to *thank* me?"

The Blight took another step toward the bed and said, "You defeated me with great skill. It is the way of the clans."

"I don't understand," said Kit.

"To reach status my people hunt game," responded the Blight. "It is an ancient custom, built on the days when we hunted each other. That is no longer done. Hasn't been done in millennia. But there is no greater honor than to fight one as skilled as you."

"Even if you lose?"

The Blight cocked his head, "The hunt is never to win. It is only to survive. Through the act of loss we learn humility. We learn perseverance. Determination."

"You fight to lose?"

"No. You misunderstand," said the Blight.

"Yea, probably," said Kit with a wry smile.

"Can I ask you," hesitated the Blight, "how is it you are so fast?"

"Fast?"

"Fast," agreed the Blight. "Almost as fast as the Masters."

"No one is that fast," said Kit. "I'm not that fast."

"You were against me. Against the rocknid too. I watch."

"I'm not that fast," said Kit again.

"You are," insisted the Blight.

"If I'm that fast, why did I lose?"

The Blight blinked at him. "You lost to learn. You lost to win."

Kit felt the soreness in his chest and winced. "That makes no sense."

The Blight scratched his head and said, "You misunderstand again."

"You sound like a friend of mine," said Kit, thinking about Ash.

"Perhaps he sounds like me," said the Blight.

"Fair enough," said Kit with a smirk.

The Blight paused and then asked, "Can I ask you something else?"

"Sure," said Kit, straightening his back despite the pain.

"Why is it you don't think your world is worth saving?"

Kit froze. "What? How did you know that?" He shook his head. "You can't know that. No one knows that."

"It is obvious," said the Blight. "If you wanted to win the games you'd fight to your full potential. You do not fight to your full potential."

"How do you know that?"

The Blight rolled a shoulder and said, "I watch."

Kit put his hand again on his chest, feeling the tightness that came with every breath.

"It will be better by tomorrow," said the Blight.

Kit looked at the Blight, staring into the creature's white on white eyes for several seconds. "There are better worlds than Earth," he said.

"They are all better worlds," said the Blight. "That which is not yours is always better."

Kit shook his head, "No. No, my people are violent. They're cruel."

The Blight rolled his shoulder again, "But that's not the reason why you hold yourself back. It runs deeper."

Kit flushed. "You don't know anything about me."

"I know about you," said the Blight.

"No you don't," said Kit, not masking his contempt. "I didn't hold myself back. I fought as hard as I could. You don't know anything about me."

"I know you are angry," said the Blight. "But not angry for losing I would think."

Kit wanted to deny it, but the words suddenly caught in his throat.

"I see it," said the Blight.

Kit took a long breath, letting it out again slowly. He hadn't realized how exhausted he felt.

"On my world there is a story," began the Blight. "It is part of the Clan Song. About a great hunter, the greatest hunter of our people, who very long ago, when he came of age, travelled to the Wild Range to kill the Bull of Heaven. No one understood why he wanted to kill the Bull of Heaven. There were many less dangerous game. But he was determined. He was stubborn. No other would do. So it was that he tracked the beast across plains and mountains, across rivers and forests. Once he nearly caught up to it, seeing its massive shadow in the distance. But every time he got to within a few kilometers, the Bull would sense him and move further and further away. And so it went for weeks and months until they had crossed the whole continent. The longer the hunt went on, so too grew his anger at the Bull." He shook his head. "He was angry at the Bull not for what he was, but for what he wasn't.

"Then," he continued, "one day as the season changed from winter to spring, the hunter found fresh tracks and realized he was only minutes behind his prey. He rushed to catch the beast, never having been so close before. He climbed one hill, and then another, and then another. At each crest he felt his hearts pound faster. But as he reached the top of the last hill he saw it: the Bull of Heaven lay dead, just having been killed by another, a wilder." The Blight suddenly raised his arms, "He flew into a rage and fell upon the wilder. He was mad with rage. They fought in the grass and in the forest and in the river. They fought and fought until the wilder lifted a rock to crush the hunter's head and realized that the hunter was no longer fighting. He realized the hunter wanted to die."

"Why did he want to die?" asked Kit.

"Because the Bull became his only reason for living," said the Blight. "Without it, he had nothing except his anger."

"That's why you fight to lose," said Kit.

"We do not fight to lose," said the Blight. "But defeat teaches us more than winning ever could."

"What happened to the hunter?"

"He and the wilder became great friends," said the Blight, his mouth contorting into something approximating a smile. "Together they unified their peoples, and in time changed the lives of generations."

"Are you the hunter or the wilder?" asked Kit.

"Neither," replied the Blight, "but I suspect you could be one or the other."

"Why me?" asked Kit.

"Because what the Masters see in you all see in you," said the Blight. "Even if you do not see it in yourself."

"I'm not anyone special," said Kit. "And besides, I lost. It's over."

"You are what you want to be," said the Blight. "You create your own reality. But first you must let go of your anger. It weighs you down. It keeps you slow."

Kit thought about his dad.

As though reading his thoughts the Blight asked: "Is there nothing good you remember?"

Kit thought about playing with his brother. Crafts with his mom. Summers with his family in Frankenmuth, Michigan. Winters at his grandma's in Hoopleton, Kansas.

"There were good things," said Kit.

"Fight for those," said the Blight.

After the Blight left his room and for a long time after, Kit was alone with his thoughts. Thoughts of home. Thoughts of the arena. Regret. He missed Ash and Bragg and hated the idea of them fighting each other. He thought about Bolts and the disappointment he must feel. He thought about his family, which he knew he'd probably never see again. But mainly he struggled against the silence. For the first time in three years he felt truly alone.

Every time he heard a creak in the floor or felt the tickle of air against his skin, he looked to the door. Hoping, against reason for Hagga the milkwoman to lumber in with a tray of food, or one of the grinders scurrying in to make repairs, or for Bolts to tell him to prepare for training. But no one came. Maybe no one would ever come again.

Later that evening, as he lay in his small bed, he suddenly realized that he could hear the unmistakable tumult of the arena from some distance above him. It was garbled by stone and metal at first, but as the volume grew it only became clearer. Soon Kit could almost make out individual voices and could feel the vibration of the clamor in his bones. He tried to imagine who might be fighting at any one moment. What they were feeling. Again his mind drifted to his friends. Even though they were his competition he felt as though he let them down somehow.

At one point he heard the unmistakable sound of booing. Jeers and anger rising so that the walls seemed to shake. But after a time it died away replaced again by the familiar noise of bloodthirsty approval.

Eventually the sounds died away. The vibrations drifted off. His room became quiet again. And again he was left with only his thoughts. So much pain. So much of it that it could fill the world. Countless worlds.

As he drifted off to sleep that night his mind flashed back to the evening a few days earlier when Bolts told him he'd picked him for the games. And he remembered the last words his Al'tkash trainer told him as he left him in his room.

"You asked me what I meant when I said you were special," Bolts had said to him.

"You said that you picked me because I could win," responded Kit.

Bolts nodded, "I didn't mean the games."

Chapter 13: Wildcard

That night Kit's dream returned.

His house in Michigan. Mom and little brother doing a craft project. Dad on the couch reading *The Collapse of the Athenian Empire,* or, *Conquerors: The Spanish Conquest of the Americas*, or, *Trinity: The Bombing of Hiroshima and Nagasaki*. A racket outside. Then out the front door. The tools gone. The project complete. A crowd gathered, even larger this time.

The workman: "Come to see what we've built? Then what are you waiting for? Go on. Go on have a look."

Again Kit hesitated.

"What are you waiting for?" asked the workman. "Go on."

Kit peeked over his shoulder to his parents and little brother standing on the stoop.

"No," he said. "No, I'm not going to do it. If I look I'll get shocked. It'll hurt."

The workman put his large mitt on Kit's shoulder and said sternly, "Then find another way."

Kit opened his eyes, shot up and clutched his forearm. He was awake. It was morning. The pain was back, like fire, now spread beyond his arm and shoulder. He felt it in his chest and stomach. In his neck and jaw. Muscles constricting. Heart pounding.

He rushed to the small bathroom off to the side of his room and emptied the contents of his stomach into the toilet. He lingered there until the pain subsided. He still didn't know what was happening to him, but it was getting worse.

For a long time that day Kit was again left only to himself. It wasn't until around midday that a small, skinny creature with downcast eyes and molting skin came into his room to deliver a bowl of cold porridge, three yellow root vegetables that resembled carrots, and something not entirely dissimilar to milk. When Kit tried to exchange some words with the creature, it quickly rushed out the door as though its life depended on it.

As the day pressed on Kit's mind drifted from sadness to boredom. To alleviate the problem first he went about systematically testing every machine in his room and figured out that most of it was medical monitoring equipment. Half a dozen machines set up to scan and analyze every molecule in a patient's body. Though from what he could tell, none of the equipment had been used in a very long time.

Once that got old he tried to mastermind a way out of his room. The Blight had done it, why shouldn't he? Unfortunately beyond the door there seemed to be no obvious way in or out and the door was solidly locked. For several hours he considered, experimented, and failed at trying to get inside the door's access panel in the hopes of reprogramming the locking mechanism, but with no tools to work with this proved impossible.

Finally as the noise of the arena above him again signaled the return of the games the door opened. Kit shot up immediately from his bed, the pain in his chest nearly gone, but still significant enough that the sudden action made him flinch.

From the doorway Phlot the overseer looked him up and down appraisingly, a look of exasperation on his large bulbous face.

"Come on," he said after a minute. "You're coming with me."

"Where?" asked Kit, suddenly unsure if he wanted to leave.

The Mog sighed. "Servants don't get to ask questions. They obey."

"I'm no servant," said Kit.

"I said let's go."

"I'm not going anywhere until you tell me where."

Anger flashed across Phlot's face, replaced almost immediately by fatigue. "You've been summoned by the Emperor."

Kit frowned. "Why would the Emperor want to see me?"

Phlot locked his jaw and then said, "Are you going to ask me a million questions I can't answer? Let's go."

Reluctantly, Kit followed the overseer out of the room and into a tight grey corridor lit up by bright pale lights from the ceiling. For a second Kit considered to ask Phlot exactly where they were going, but as they walked on he thought better of it.

The corridor was tight, with doors evenly spaced every dozen meters. Kit imagined that behind the doors were rooms like his, each one home to a vanquished fighter. Then Kit thought about the rocknid trying to squeeze through the cramped corridor and decided the creature must have special accommodations elsewhere.

Phlot led Kit to a set of stairs and the two of them started up without comment. In fact the overseer didn't so much as glance back behind him. *I could run*, Kit thought. Egg had taught him to fly most standard starships in stasis. If he could get to a spaceport he might have a chance to make it back to Earth.

It was a stupid idea, he knew. Even if he somehow managed to leave the coliseum, and somehow find a ship, and then somehow to launch it, he knew he'd most likely never get past the orbital defense grid. Besides, going to Earth would be pointless. Soon there'd be nothing to go back to.

After three flights they stepped out onto a wide-open floor of polished marble and white tree columns rising out of the floor to spread their branches of silver leaves into the high ceiling. Here the noise of the coliseum was inescapable, as cheers and jeers, clapping and stomping melted together into a din that permeated everything.

Phlot walked past the tree columns and around a curve to a large set of ornate silver doors, flanked by two golden armored Champions, each with a long, etched spear. Neither gave them any notice.

"All right, now you listen," said Phlot, turning to Kit a few steps from the doors. "You bow to the Lord Emperor, deep and low. You do not speak unless spoken to. And if you show any disrespect, gods help you, for I'll tear you to pieces myself. You understand?"

Kit nodded, suddenly feeling a knot form in his stomach.

The overseer gave him a long look, frowned at him, sighed, and then turned back to the doors. For several minutes they waited.

From what Kit knew of the Masters, and especially the royal court, it was a rare thing indeed for a fighter to meet personally with the Lord Emperor. There were many levels of separation in place. It was the reason why overseers like Phlot existed.

As the anxiety Kit was feeling spiked, there was the sound of metal on metal and suddenly the ornate doors swung open. He wasn't sure what he had expected to see on the other side, but the sight of Ash nearly knocked him flat.

"What are you doing here?" is what he wanted to ask, but the words wouldn't come. All Kit could do was stare helplessly as Ash ran up to him and threw her arms around his neck. Kit returned the embrace, and for the few seconds that it lasted, nothing in the universe could have felt better.

Kit was about to try and ask her again what she was doing there, but before he could, Ash's trainer appeared from behind her and hurriedly pulled them apart. All he could do was watch helplessly as she was pushed away from him, a sad smile on her lips.

Then, to Kit's surprise, Tau came out through the doors accompanied by his trainer, the pigment in his skin dancing wildly, a scowl across his face. For a moment their eyes met. "You're dead," the craftee seemed to say.

"Come on then," said Phlot, giving Kit a hard shove in the back.

Kit glanced over his shoulder and watched as Ash and Tau, escorted by their trainers, were led away in the direction of the stairs.

"What's going on?" asked Kit.

"Shut your mouth," whispered Phlot. "You're in the presence of royalty."

They stepped through the doorway and into a large multi-level suite, of marble and tree pillars, luxuriously adorned with tapestries, rugs, divans, and couches. Kit realized instantly where he was, as to his left was a wall made entirely of glass overlooking the coliseum interior, and at its center a set of doors leading out onto the Emperor's eight-pillared pavilion, occupied by the royal court. Beyond that a boisterous crowd, cheering wildly as an elephant like creature devoured a hapless slave in the arena below.

After the ornate silver doors closed behind them with a loud thud, Kit realized that he and Phlot were not the only ones in the lavish suite. Opposite the glass wall and arena, under a large computer display, just near a long table filled with food and drink from across the galaxy, stood three figures. First, was Lord Emperor Aejus'lobine, tall and slender, dressed in a dark blue tunic, and jacket with silver accents and a circlet atop his head. Next to him stood another Master, the priestess who had given the opening invocation, cracked skin, and dim light beneath a silver robe. And third, off to the side was Bolts, black on black eyes regarding him silently.

Kit couldn't help a smile at the sight of his trainer.

For a moment the two Masters chatted quietly amongst themselves, as though no one else were in the room, the Lord Emperor snacking on some delicacy from off the banquet table, while the priestess whispered something to him, gesturing lightly with her hand. Then, a few moments later, as though noticing them for the first time, the priestess glanced over at Kit and smiled.

A couple more words were exchanged. The priestess gave a short bow to the Emperor, who seemed disinterested by everything around him, and then as though floating on air, the priestess glided over to Kit, her long robe rippling behind her.

She came to within half a meter of him, looming over both him and Phlot as though a giant. For a moment she looked down at Kit, and Kit looked up at her, the smile on her face never wavering. Then suddenly, she leaned down and took Kit's chin in her large, broken hand. Her skin was as hard and cold as stone. Kit did his best to fight the urge to break free.

"Human," she said as though to someone else, turning his head with her hand.

Kit wasn't sure if she wanted a response from him.

"We've observed humans for many thousand years," she continued after a beat. "Not a particularly significant species save for their propensity for violence. Why should humans attain ascension?"

It took Kit a moment to realize that she was in fact addressing him.

"I don't know," was all he could think to say.

"Pity," she replied.

She let go of his face, leaving his cheeks stinging and smiled softly at him.

"There were those who thought the human world should have been destroyed," she said casually. "Did you know that? Some still do. Makes no matter. It can happen still. Not all vanquished worlds are offered the blessing of servitude. Servitude is a gift, you see?"

Kit again was struck silent.

The priestess studied him and then said, "Primitive. Ugly. Savage."

Kit locked his jaw.

The priestess continued: "Your fate was written. But the gods have other plans for you."

"I don't understand," he said.

Her smile widened with amusement. "No of course you don't," she said.

Kit glanced over at Bolts, still off to the side. His trainer said nothing. No flicker of thought crossed his face.

"Must you torture the poor creature?" came the voice of the Lord Emperor, as with a blood red drink in hand he crossed the room and plopped himself down on a large, plush couch. "Let me see him."

The priestess took a last lingering look at Kit and retreated a few steps. Suddenly Phlot smacked Kit in the back and they both stepped toward the Emperor, then both overseer and fighter bowed low and deep.

"What do they call you?" asked the Lord Emperor. "Kopper is it?"

"Kit," said Kit, as he and Phlot stood straight again.

"You were quite the amusement, Kopper," said the Lord Emperor as though not hearing him. "Yes, quite the amusement indeed. I do believe that your fight against that giant rock creature was the most talked about spectacle in centuries. Quite an achievement, I needn't tell you, when you consider the vast number of matches that have taken place in this hallowed arena."

Kit felt another smack across his back from Phlot and blurted out, "Thank you."

The Lord Emperor smiled broadly, the gesture adding contrast to his already boney, blue cheeks. "Tell me, Kopper," he said, taking a sip of his drink, "do you believe that you deserve a second chance?"

Kit frowned and again glanced to Bolts.

"I don't understand," he said turning back to the Emperor.

Aejus'lobine sighed and to the priestess said, "These lesser species are so damned thick. Might as well be speaking to an armchair."

The priestess chortled and said, "Poor genetics I'm afraid. The Science Ministry has sent Your Majesty numerous reports on the declining biological quality of newly discovered species."

"Yes, yes, yes," said the Lord Emperor as he took a sip from his glass.

Back to Kit: "Do you deserve a second chance to compete in the games? It's a simple question, either you do or you don't. Makes no matter to us, although the people shall be amused and we must amuse the people." His eyes drifted. "You did make quite the impression on them." He leaned in, his dark eyes piercing. "You made quite an impression on our court as well," he said almost at a whisper.

For a moment the Lord Emperor held Kit's gaze and then leaned back again on his couch, taking another sip of his drink, just as a massive roar went up from the crowd in the coliseum.

"They love their spectacle," said Aejus'lobine, as he took a dispassionate glance out at the crowd. "The greater the spectacle the happier the mob. And if the mob is happy, the Empire is happy."

"Our objection stands," interjected the priestess.

The Lord Emperor, seeming bemused replied to the priestess, "We know all about your objections on both this species and the masses, but I remind our distinguished emissary of the gods that we are the power in the galaxy. That although the gods are everlasting, the good cheer of the populace is not."

The priestess bowed her head, but added: "Our objection stands, Your Majesty."

Aejus'lobine took another sip of his glass chalice and seemed to consider something for a moment as he looked at the priestess, the silver veins under his skin glowing in rhythm with his pulse.

"There's been a lot of talk about humans," he said, finally turning back to Kit. "Some good and some bad, but overall human ascension is favored by at least half our court." He shot a look back at the priestess, then again to Kit. "I needn't tell you whom the other half favors. And we can certainly continue as is and in time the disappointment will fade. But, then these games might be robbed of the kind of grand finale they deserve. Gods remember the disaster that was the Great Kneeling."

He took in a breath and let it out just as slowly. "No, spectacle must be served," he continued. "The factions must be satisfied. gods know that if we left anything to chance a creature as primitive as the Optwap could win." He turned to the priestess. "Can you imagine? That *thing* winning ascension?"

The priestess laughed, although seemingly without any sincerity.

"So, human," said the Lord Emperor again back to Kit. "We will declare a wildcard melee. It is not without precedent, happens every few hundred years. And even if there was no precedent, what does it matter?" He smirked slightly. "You and a selection of vanquished fighters, white and black, will get a second chance to compete in the games. Which means, you'll face the same creature that killed you. If you win, you'll get to compete against the finalist for ascension. If you lose," he shrugged, "well, then you'll have the honor to serve. What do you say to that?"

Kit frowned and asked, "What about my friends?"

The Lord Emperor burst out in laughter. "Oh, what a delight!"

"This type of impertinence is a precisely why we are concerned," said the priestess. "If we may–"

Suddenly the Lord Emperor threw his chalice on the marble floor, the glass shattering in an explosion of crystal and liquid.

"That's enough!" he shouted at the priestess. "We've made our decision and it is final. We will hear not another word of it!"

The priestess lowered her head and said not another word, while Phlot brushed glass shards off his arm.

Aejus'lobine closed his eyes a moment and took in a long breath. Then opening them again he said to Kit: "As you can see there is much passion surrounding your kind's ascension. For the first time in our history even those who would fight you have pled for you." His eyes drifted to the figures sitting on the pavilion outside. "There is much division. And we aim to eliminate it."

The Lord Emperor looked back to Kit, his smile suddenly back on his face. "Make a good show in the melee," he said, "win the tournament, and we'll see who's right and who's wrong."

With that the Lord Emperor stood. Phlot again smacked Kit on the back and again they both bowed deep and long. The priestess took an appraising look at Kit, and then without a word both Masters walked out through the glass doors, back into the roaring coliseum. As they passed the air seemed to grow colder.

After it was over, Phlot looked over at Bolts and said, "He's yours again." Then to Kit: "For the time being."

The overseer turned and strode out of the room via the ornate silver doors. And like that Kit and his trainer were alone.

"What happened?" asked Kit.

Bolts remained silent for a moment and then crossed the room to Kit, kneeling down to meet his eyes. "I was worried about you," he said, placing a hand on Kit's shoulder. "There was concern the damage was too extensive even for the nano. I'm happy they were wrong."

Kit was shocked into silence. In all the years they'd known each other, Kit had never known Bolts to express anything resembling emotion.

"We better go," said Bolts, "we have to prepare. A melee is extremely dangerous."

Kit shook off his shock and said, "I don't understand what happened."

"Division among the royal court. Those who favor human ascension tipped the scale in your favor." He hesitated then added, "But I think that your friend made the difference. She threatened to forfeit if you weren't allowed a second chance."

Kit felt a tightening in his chest. Ash had fought for him. She risked her worlds for him.

"Why would she do that?" asked Kit. "If I win her world is lost."

Bolts looked down to the floor a moment and replied, "She knows her world is already lost. As the Lord Emperor said, only two fighters are favored for ascension."

And all at once Kit understood. It was as Egg had told him. The game was rigged. The Masters had decreed that only he or Tau could win. And Kit knew that Tau would do anything to win.

As pain, anger, love, and relief washed over him, Kit asked, "Why me?"

"They see something in humans," responded Bolts. "Something they can exploit."

"They think we're like them."

"You'll never be like them."

Kit nodded. Despite himself he still wasn't sure.

"What happens now?" he asked as Bolts stood and they began walking out of the room.

Bolts looked at him sidelong and replied, "You fight. You win."

***

The schedule had changed. The fight between Tau and Ash was postponed from that evening to the next to immediately precede the melee. From what Kit heard after the fact, the initial disappointment of those in attendance and those lucky enough to watch the action live across the link worlds, was immediately relieved by the details of the match to follow.

"There will be six of you in the arena at the same time," Bolts told him. "Three white, three black. The last one standing will go on to the finale."

That was two fighters more than had ever been known in the history of the melee. And despite what might have been claimed, the participants weren't chosen on points, or merit, or any such thing, but purely, obviously, for entertainment value.

On black he'd face both the rocknid and the Optwap for a second time. His fight with the rocknid was still being replayed on the link. While the Optwap's defeat to Tau was now being described as "the most thrilling semi-final in the history of the games."

On white, Kit would meet for the first time the tall, skinless Tobrus, a master with a long sword, and an insectoid from a planet called Mrith, a being resembling an upright, armored spider, who, like the Optwap, favored his own natural gifts over a weapon. In this case, a set of four razor sharp claws and vice-like mandibles. Finally, rounding out the white team, was Bragg.

"In the arena you'll have no friends," Bolts had told him. "Remember that above all else."

Kit wondered if he'd be able to fight Bragg when the time came. More than anything he hoped he wouldn't have to find out.

That evening the atmosphere throughout the coliseum was electric. Tension and fear below, excitement and anticipation above. There hadn't been a melee battle in the games for centuries, the last having been so brutal that according to Bolts the ascended species still talked about it with a sort of silent reverence.

"Remember," said Bolts, kneeling down in front of him as they prepared to go, "be quick and be aware of your surroundings at all times."

Kit nodded and placed his helmet on his head.

"If I don't win-" he began to say.

"You will," said Bolts firmly. "Your journey doesn't end here."

His trainer then put his hand over the patch on Kit's shoulder and for a moment closed his eyes. If Bolts was praying, Kit didn't think to ask.

Stepping out into the arena was like walking into the eye of a hurricane. The stands were filled beyond capacity, rippling like an organic wave with hundreds of thousands of beings, on their feet, all screaming. As Kit made his way out of a small side entrance to one of the six start pads, he glanced at the royal party sitting on their couches in their columned pavilion. Lord Emperor Aejus'lobine stared at him, eyes piercing, half smiling.

Three of the other fighters were already in their places waiting: the rocknid, looking as overwhelmed as he had during their last bought; the Tobrus, who regarded him coolly by his lidless, yellow eyes; and the Optwap, mouth contorted into a snarl, body tensed up as though it would leap at Kit from halfway across the arena at any moment.

As Kit stepped onto his pad, the light beneath him turning green, he noticed that there was only one gravity well set up for the melee. It was placed directly in the center of the arena, immediately below three levels of immobile platforms, counting nine in total.

Although difficult to perceive amidst the continuous roar of the crowd, there was a marked uptick in volume as the insectoid from Mrith and Kit's friend Bragg stepped onto the arena floor. Kit wished he could say something to Bragg before the fight. Exchange a word, shake one of his friend's hands, but Bragg didn't so much as glance in his direction. *Probably for the best*, Kit thought.

There were no speeches. No introductions. No fanfare. The moment they were all on their start pads the countdown started.

...8, 7, 6...

For the last three years Kit had trained in single combat, now he was facing five fighters each with a completely unique fighting style. Two of whom he'd never seen in action before. He wasn't prepared. How could he be in just a day? But Kit was glad in the knowledge that his competition was equally disadvantaged. It wasn't much of a comfort, but it was better than nothing. As he looked at each fighter in turn, he could sense their apprehension. Even the Optwap, wild and hungry, seemed momentarily cowed by the uncertainty of what was about to come next.

...5, 4, 3...

For his part, Bolts didn't make Kit train any new techniques or last minute strategies. The melee would be chaos. A bloody free-for-all. The best way for Kit to survive was to stay light on his feet and keep aware of his surroundings. The first several minutes would be the most crucial, as everyone rushed to take out as much of the competition as possible. The best way to make it through would be to avoid combat altogether at first, barring that, to limit contact to one fighter at a time. Kit glanced at the rocknid, swaying in place, threatening to step off his start pad at any moment. The rocknid was the key. Hardest to kill and most unpredictable. If Kit could use him to his advantage somehow, he might have a chance.

...2, 1, FIGHT!

The surge that shot through his muscles was more intense than anything he'd ever felt before. Just as waking from his dream had become ever more painful, so too now was the sensation in his bones and flesh as his heart beat quickened and adrenaline washed through him. And as the last of the discomfort left him, he noticed once again a perceptible slowing in time. The fighters, the cheering spectators, all moved in slow motion. Downtempo and plodding. But something was different. Was he moving slightly faster? It wasn't much, barely perceptible, perhaps exaggerated given his heightened awareness, but to Kit it seemed as though his grip were lighter, as though the movement of his arms and legs easier.

There was no time to stop and ponder.

Kit glanced up and noticed the other fighters already in motion. The rocknid, was halfway through a swing at the skinless swordsman from Tobra. The insectoid was rushing Bragg, the other's short swords at the ready. And the Optwap? Dodging past the rocknid, barely avoiding a swing from the Tobrus, the Optwap was heading straight for Kit, its teeth glistening. Kit took several steps back and raised his sword to meet him. The Optwap leapt, claws striking hot against hypnotic steel. The force knocked them both down and sent them sliding.

Kit jumped to his feet, surprised by how quickly he managed it, and swung for the beast's midsection. The Optwap yelped as the blade made contact and fur and blood exploded in a mist between them. The Optwap sprang back and then again forward, roaring at Kit, swiping at his face. Kit sidestepped, swung again, just barely missing a second chance to finish the Optwap right there and then.

For several minutes they were locked in a vicious back and forth. Straining, fighting relentlessly. A blaze of steel and claws and teeth. Everything around them melted away and Kit found himself fighting the match he should have fought three days earlier. Clear headed. Fast. In a fury.

Then the abrupt, unmistakable sound of a rock slide behind him made Kit turn and jump instinctively, as a massive spiked mace came down where he had just been standing, breaking several floor plates with a loud crash. Kit rolled and bounced back to his feet as the rocknid charged, taking a swing at the Optwap, forcing the creature to momentarily forget his previous target.

Kit looked to the other side of the arena. Bragg was now engaged with the skinless swordsman, barely keeping up with the other's mad swings, and incredible reach, but somehow managing to keep his own. It was at that moment that Kit noticed the insectoid, jumping down at him from one of the platforms floating some distance above him. Kit dodged the landing, and impaling by a sharp claw, and countered with a sword thrust at the creature's thorax. The swing missed, and the insectoid jabbed at him once, twice, three more times. Kit blocked, countered, blocked again, one eye on the insectoid, another on everyone else.

The insectoid was good, powerful, but ultimately predictable. His move set was formulaic. Upper right jab, upper left jab, strike with mandibles. Lower right thrust, lower left thrust, strike with mandibles. But while his attack pattern was lazy his broader strategy of forcing Kit back into the attack zone of the rocknid was smart. If Kit hadn't been so highly aware of his surroundings it might have even worked. Kit let the insectoid push him back a few meters and then rushed him, forcing him to pull aside to avoid the thrust of his sword. Kit spun them both around and took another swing at him. It was barely deflected, but managed to throw the insectoid off his balance.

From what Kit remembered of Egg's lessons the insectoids of Mrith were mainly builders. Few in number, but with lifespans into the hundreds of years, they constructed gigantic maze-like cities just below the surface of their one vast, albeit barren continent. Sections were millennia old and stored the insectoid's most important relics: great data wheels on which were recorded tens of thousands of years of knowledge. Egg had once played for Kit a sampling of the insectoid's music. Kit had never heard anything so beautiful in all his life.

Kit pushed in more aggressively against the insectoid. He swung his blade again and again, each time taking a step toward his adversary. Low. High. Midsection. Head. He became a blur of hypnotic steel. Limbs moving as though in a rhythm. All the space around him flashing. The insectoid took three steps back. And another. And another. And another. Swings wild. He blocked all he could. Limbs flailing, trying to keep up.

As the insectoid stumbled, Kit pressed harder. Faster. He became like a whirlwind. Free form and automated. His mind rising above his body. Aware of all things, computing distance, strength, pacing. He slashed at the insectoid. Harder with every point of contact. Unrestrained in his brutality.

Then all of a sudden Kit stopped his attack.

The insectoid froze, and looked at him for a split second curiously, as though unable to make sense of what had just happened, when suddenly a massive spiked mace came down on him like a falling star. The impact was seismic and utterly destroyed the insectoid in an explosion of limbs and blood. The rocknid howled triumphantly as a voice over the loudspeaker announced the defeat of the fighter from Mrith.

There was no time to pause. As the annihilation of the insectoid sent a wave of excitement through the crowd, Kit found himself again under renewed attack by the Optwap. It was coming on more aggressively now, forcing Kit on the defense. He was back peddling, blocking, blocking, blocking. The rocknid took notice of them both, and as Kit fought off the Optwap the rocknid rushed to take swings at them both.

For several long moments the battle became a rapid series of violent exchanges, sword, claw, and teeth, while stone feet and spiked maces created craters around them. The Optwap leapt at Kit, recoiled, sprang back from off the rocknid's arm, snapped, retreated, through the rocknid's legs, slashing at him, tearing at his battle suit. Kit for his part dodged, moving constantly, circling, looking for an opportunity to fall back, regroup. The rocknid became increasingly furious. Screaming a sound like rocks in a blender as each attack just narrowly missed to make contact.

Patience, Kit reminded himself. *Look for an opportunity.*

It took a few more circuits, a few more near misses, but the opportunity came as the Optwap leapt for Kit again, although this time just a little too slowly. As it jumped, jaws parted, the rocknid turned his massive arm and caught the Optwap midair. It wasn't enough to knock it out of the fight, but it was enough to knock it halfway across the arena, shrieking.

Kit braced and ran in the opposite direction, for the center of the arena, and saw Bragg, a few meters from the gravity well, down on the floor, barely withstanding the skinless swordsman's onslaught with his one remaining blade.

The planet Tobra was a dark world, a solitary planet circling a faint star, made tropical by a superheated core. The skinless people who dwelled on its surface were a highly secretive species that constructed vast astronomical maps that were the basis for their religious worship. Highly advanced, these experts in cosmic cartography had already achieved interstellar travel by the time they were discovered by the Masters. According to Egg the people of Tobra had developed a kind of galactic mysticism that might very well hold the answers to every mystery in the universe.

When Kit barreled into the skinless Tobrus, he sent him sliding nearly twenty meters. A stream of blue blood gushing out of the wound where Kit had stabbed him.

"Thank you," said Bragg, breathless, as an announcement declared the Tobrus out of the competition.

Kit smirked at his friend as he helped him up, "We're not out of this yet."

Bragg picked up one of his short swords from off the floor and said, "You have plan?"

Kit gestured to the platforms, "Height is our advantage."

Bragg nodded and they both ran.

They reached the gravity well just as the Optwap was coming to within striking distance. Bragg hopped on first, Kit went second. The effect wasn't quite what he'd expected.

Instead of being deposited on the same platform, Kit found himself on the second tier, with Bragg on the third. To make matters worse, the platforms began to move the moment they landed. The whole thing worked like some sort of floating puzzle, where platforms shifted vertically and horizontally, rearranging themselves at random. They'd remain in one position for a few heartbeats and then move again to create a different arrangement altogether.

Despite the randomness of the platforms the Optwap was on Kit in seconds. As the beast pounced, nearly knocking Kit over the edge, a nearby platform exploded as the rocknid smashed it with one of his spiked maces from below.

This is familiar, thought Kit as he got back to his feet, slashing at the Optwap to force him back a step.

They fought again. Claws, jaws, blade. Strike and counter, dodge and block. Back and forth on one small moving platform. It was seconds but seemed to go on forever. And then Kit heard his friend Bragg shouting.

The rocknid's mace came up from beneath. At a heightened state of perception, Kit watched as the platform they were standing on slowly broke open from its center, a row of spikes lifting the middle and then tearing it as though it were a sheet of paper. In a fraction of a second there would be nothing beneath him but splinters and a long fall to the arena floor.

Kit jumped, just barely grabbing hold of a nearby platform with his one free hand. Below him the rocknid raised his maces, visibly angry, as debris rained down around him. And then Kit felt hot breath on the skin of his fingers. He looked up. Just above his head was the Optwap, leering down at him, mouth twisted in a sort of grin, saliva dripping from its fangs. Death by Optwap above, death by rocknid below. Kit almost felt like laughing.

And suddenly, there came Bragg. Jumping from about four meters above he fell onto the Optwap, just missing driving his swords into the creature's back. The blade took a good slice out of the Optwap's side, splattering blood across them both as the creature sprang away in retreat.

Bragg took ahold of Kit by two free hands and pulled him up.

"Thanks," said Kit.

"We are even," said Bragg.

As the platforms shifted again, putting some distance between them and the Optwap, Bragg smacked Kit on the back and said, "You fight. You win."

As he began to turn, Kit grabbed the other boy by an arm. "What are you talking about?"

Bragg glanced down at the rocknid, already repositioning himself below them, readying another strike with his mace, and said, "I will not win, but you have a chance. No time." He smiled. "Now I use your trick."

Before Kit could stop him, Bragg stepped off the platform and dropped down onto the rocknid, grabbing onto his head with his two free hands, stabbing wildly with his swords. The rocknid panicked, screaming so loudly that it drowned out the roar of the crowd. Dropping his maces he started swatting at Bragg trying to get him off. Pounding at him with his massive hands. Somehow, despite crushing blow after crushing blow Bragg clung onto the rocknid, stabbing his blades. Slicing through the rocknid's armor to the soft tissue below.

It lasted mere seconds, but when it was over both fighters collapsed. Bragg first, bruised, bloody, bones broken. The rocknid fell immediately after. The armored giant wavering, then stumbling, and finally falling, covered in black tar blood.

An announcement echoed through the coliseum. Only two fighters remained. Suddenly all the platforms moved together, creating one large, continuous surface, floating four meters above the arena floor. The Optwap was already rushing at Kit with a renewed determination. Kit tightened the grip on his sword and raised his blade. He thought about Bragg. It was time to finish this once and for all.

For Kit it was hard to know how long they fought. It seemed to go on forever, although in truth it was probably just minutes. The Optwap came at him as though possessed, trying to rip him into pieces with its claws and teeth. But unlike in their previous fight, Kit was in complete control. With the world at half speed and his senses enhanced, he could anticipate the Optwap's every move, counter its every attack.

Their battle was a dance, sparks, as claws met blade, exploding between them. When the Optwap found an opening it rushed. When the Optwap rushed, Kit sidestepped. The Optwap would bristle and follow. Rinse. Repeat. A dozen times, maybe more.

It wasn't long before the Optwap started growing weaker, its attacks coming slower, its charges less powerful. It was panting slightly, his tongue inching out from between its fangs. Soon it started making mistakes. Its strikes weren't connecting as frequently. *Don't underestimate your opponent,* his trainer's words appearing in Kit's mind. *At his weakest an opponent can be most dangerous.*

Careful to keep out of the Optwap's range, Kit started to circle around it, deflecting its attacks as they came, waiting for the perfect chance to finish him. As he moved the Optwap turned with him, growling, biting at the air.

Slowly, Kit thought. *Carefully.*

The Optwap jumped at him, going for his neck. Kit dodged, cutting the creature across its leg as he swept past. The Optwap, landed with a yelp, some blood splattering as it did, and reared to jump again. But this time Kit moved first. Feigning left, he turned right cutting with his blade up as he moved. The sword caught the Optwap below the jaw, opening its throat just a little.

The Optwap doubled back, baring its teeth, but Kit was on him again. He slashed at its legs, then at its head, then toward its chest. At first the creature seemed as though it might resist the onslaught, but again its obvious fatigue worked against it. Kit pushed in. He cut the Optwap across the arm. Pushed in again and cut the Optwap across the abdomen. Pushed in a third time, cutting the other leg. And as the Optwap lost its footing, Kit drove his blade into the creature's chest.

The Optwap jerked, shuddered, and collapsed to the floor, a last groan escaping his mouth. For barely a second, everything seemed absolutely still. And suddenly Kit realized the fight was over. Just like that the fighter that had defeated him three days earlier now lay at his feet in a pool of its own blood. This time Kit let himself feel the satisfaction of victory. If that made him monstrous he didn't care.

As he retracted his blade, an announcement declared: "Winner of the melee, Kopper Io Talos, Earth."

Kit looked out over the coliseum. The crowds, swelling, standing, were going wild with excitement. At least for now, in this fleeting instant, he was their champion. The applause lasted nearly twenty minutes.

186 **kp dawes**

Chapter 14: The Convergence

"Who are you?" asked Kit.

"I'm you," replied the other.

"Then who am I?"

If Kit was the convergence, then he was much like the center of a disc, still, in the center of all things. And as though tied by string, all things connected back to him and only to him. A trillion, trillion living, thinking beings, some entering, some leaving, some waking, some dreaming. All back to him. Sound and soul.

Kit knew, though he did not know how he knew it, that even in that moment seven dozen interstellar wars raged across the known galaxy. Famines, pandemics, and ecological collapse reduced populations on over a hundred worlds. Fifteen major civilizations were experiencing a golden age. At least double that were in the midst of apocalypse. On hundreds of worlds prophets rose, rulers fell, revolutions burned. One sentient, advanced, species was at that moment going through an extinction event, the last member of which would perish the following weekend.

Stars churned like furnaces. Planets spun their orbits. Singularities deconstructed matter. The Dark Unknown continued its slow, deliberate expansion.

And back on Earth, life continued as it always had. A great many people died, some violently. A great number of people lived, some happily. Mostly people got by from one day to the next. They worked. They worried about school, and money, and family. They played games, read books, watched television. They played sports. They prayed. They fell in and out of love. Not one was the wiser, at least not with any certainty, that they were not alone in the universe. And not one among them had the slightest inclination that at that very moment, their fate, and the fate of everyone they knew, was being decided on a faraway alien world. Not one among them knew that their lives were in the hands of a kid from Michigan.

"You are the convergence," replied his double, a sly smirk growing across his face. "You are the cosmic center."

"What does that mean?" asked Kit.

"It's not something that I can tell you," he said. "It's something you'll have to see."

And as Kit fought Tau, the boy from a crafted world called Ifis, he saw. He saw everything. Earth, Nos, Bolts, Egg, the Lord Emperor, his dad. He could see the defeat of the Highborne and the spinning rings of the World Ship. He could feel the pulse of the trillions of beings across the link worlds and those beyond. He could see himself standing on the First World, the Temple, the light of a billion stars lighting the sky afire. And darkness. And sleep. For a thousand, thousand years.

He thought about Ash and the collective memory of generations of his ancestors stored in the blood coursing through his veins. And as the seconds began to stretch and time to slow, he imagined a life without the Masters, a galaxy at peace. *Is this what I'm fighting for?* he thought. *Is this why I'm here?*

He'd been distraught at finding Tau in the barracks after his triumph in the melee, even though he'd known to expect it. Not because he was afraid to fight Tau but because he was sad for Ash. She who was his friend. Who was so certain that her people would never be enslaved. She had lost everything and somehow, improbably, he had not.

"Can I see her? Can I go talk to her?" he asked his trainer.

Bolts only shook his head, as he ran checks on Kit, accessing his implant, monitoring his vitals. "She's not your concern right now. Only your next match matters." He glanced back at his screen, his face expressionless and asked, "Are you feeling alright?"

Kit inhaled a sharp breath and said, "I want to see her. She deserves more than-"

"This isn't about what anyone deserves," said Bolts, cutting him off. "The odds were stacked against her as was. Now you have an opportunity to end this. Put your energy there."

As Bolts went back to his screen, tabulating results, sifting through hundreds of lines of information, Kit quietly fumed. But he wasn't angry with his trainer, not even with Tau. For the first time he was angry with the Masters. Obviously it had always been the Masters, but Kit had never felt it so personally before.

"How are you feeling?" asked Bolts again.

That night, Kit's dream changed again.

The house in Michigan. Mom and little brother doing a craft project. Dad on the couch reading *Resistance and Betrayal: The History of the Warsaw Uprising,* or, *While the World Sleeps: Genocide and Conflict in Modern Africa*, or, *Dark Horizon: How Our Technology is Doomed to Destroy Us*. Suddenly there was a racket outside. Kit crossed the living room and went out the front door.

Outside, the tools, along with most of the workmen were gone. The project was complete. A crowd of spectators had gathered. It seemed like the whole town had come out, but among the throngs were aliens too. The other fighters, their trainers. Ash, Bragg, Bolts. All slaves, no masters.

The large workman with black skin, heavy gut in checkered shirt, and grey stubble on his face, smiled at Kit as he approached. "Come to see what we've built?" he asked. "Then what are you waiting for? Go on. Go on have a look."

Kit stopped as he had before. He already knew how this would play out.

"What are you waiting for?" asked the workman. "Go on."

Kit peeked over his shoulder to his parents and little brother standing on the stoop. And then he noticed something he hadn't noticed before.

"What is that?" he asked as he approached his brother.

The boy grinned at him and hurriedly glanced up at their mother.

"You can show him," she said with a nod. "It's for him."

"It's for you," said his brother barely able to contain his excitement.

Kit looked down and beheld his sword, hypnotic blue blade, silver grip and guard, in his brother's small hand.

"We made it," announced his brother proudly. "We made it for you!"

With a nod of encouragement from their mom, Kit carefully accepted the sword. As he lifted the blade, as though learning its balance for the first time his dad raised his brows at him, "Are you going to just swing that thing around or do you planning on using it?"

He didn't need to be told what to do. He knew. Somehow he knew. Without a word to his brother or parents, or the workman, who stood with arms crossed seeming to approve of what would happen next, Kit walked the few steps back to the construction. He hesitated for only a moment, licking his lips, feeling a sudden nervousness, until he raised his sword and slashed the sheeting, once, twice, three times across.

No spark. No shock. No Rodney Richter or Chris Caputo. Not this time. The covers shred and began to fall harmlessly, pulling more of the plastic with them, unwrapping the scaffolding like an onion. Layer by layer, round and round. And as the plastic fell so too did the metal girders holding them up. Plastic, metal, and wood, cracked, splintered, all peeled away and crashed onto the grass. The crowd stirred. Whispers filled the air. The anticipation thick. Until before long there was nothing left standing of the scaffolding but the thing that had been at its center. Kit blinked. He stepped back. The thing that had been at its center was him.

For several heartbeats Kit stared at Kit, eyes wide, mouth open. His double, dressed in his black battlesuit, though without the helmet, stared back at him, an amused though not unfriendly smile across his face. For several moments there was only deafening silence.

"Who are you?" finally asked Kit.

"I'm you," replied the other without missing a beat.

It was a vague, though certainly obvious answer. So he decided to try again.

"Then who am I?" asked Kit.

His double seemed to consider the question for a moment. He cocked his head, brushed a few strands of his dark hair away from his dark eyes, before he finally said: "You are the convergence. You are the cosmic center." A sly smirk spread across his face.

Kit planted his sword in the ground and asked: "What does that mean?"

His double considered this question for a moment as well before replying: "It's not something that I can tell you. It's something you'll have to see."

Kit locked his jaw. "Who are you?"

As the crowd stirred again, his double let out a light chuckle and took several steps toward Kit, stepping over the debris of the scaffolding.

"I'm you," he said, coming to within arm's reach of Kit. "You're me. And we are everything."

"The convergence," said Kit, still uncertain of the meaning.

"The convergence," agreed his double as he raised his hand.

Kit flinched slightly at which his double stopped short of making contact and said, "Do you really think I would hurt me?"

Kit raised his chin, stared himself in the eye and replied, "No I guess not."

His double smiled at him again and put his hand on his shoulder. "Now I want you to open your eyes and *see*."

Kit opened his eyes, shot up and clutched his shoulder. He was awake. It was morning. The pain was back, like fire, but this time it was everywhere. He felt it in his arms, legs, stomach, chest, and even in his head. Especially in his head. Like a red-hot poker going through his skull right where he had his implant.

Muscles constricting. Vision blurred. Heart pounding. He tried to stand and failed. His legs wouldn't support his weight. Didn't even want to move at his command. He tried to stand a second time. He managed to sit up, but almost immediately fell back down again. The pain was more intense than it had ever been before.

For a long time he lay in bed, concentrating on his breathing, trying to will himself better. Eventually he did get better. Slowly the pain left him. Out from his core, from his head and arms and legs until it barely remained just in his toes and fingertips. Only then did he let himself sit up. Then stand. He felt sick. Drained. Disoriented. But he didn't run to the bathroom this time.

"The convergence," he said aloud. "The convergence," he said again. "The convergence," he said a third time.

He stood still, allowing his strength to return, thinking less about his dream and more about seeing what it was his double wanted him to see. But how was he to see it? Where and how should he look?

Kit didn't tell Bolts about the dream. He didn't tell him about the pain. He didn't tell him about being the convergence, whatever that meant. All the same his trainer seemed to know something was different. He eyed Kit all throughout their training session, glancing at the screen in his hand, occasionally making a note.

Time seemed to have no meaning that last day of the games. Moments drifted in and out. Seconds seemed to hang frozen, and then suddenly Kit would blink and whole hours had gone. He felt lightheaded. Out of his element. Out of all elements. Floating in a world not of this world. Did he even eat breakfast or lunch? He couldn't remember. Had he spoken to Bolts at all that day? Had he spoken to anyone at all? The sensation was one of having stared at the shadows on a wall all his life, and then suddenly turning around and seeing the light. Nothing mattered and yet everything mattered.

That evening as he and Tau stood with their trainers in front of the doors leading to the Hall of Champions, Phlot tapping his foot impatiently, waiting for the start of the final round, Kit's vision suddenly blurred. And when a few moments later his focused returned he was no longer in the barracks. Tau, Bolts, Phlot, everyone was gone and before him instead of the large doors leading to the Hall of Champions and the coliseum beyond, was a lush valley full of living, breathing greenery. In the valley among the winding rivers and grasses and animals were a series of massive trees, bigger than any trees Kit had ever seen, except they weren't trees.

"It's a city," said his friend Egg, but Kit knew it wasn't really Egg.

"This is Ifis," said Kit as he watched a great flight of birds circle the massive city of brown and green trunks.

"The city Kifau on the planet Ifis," agreed Egg. "The homeworld of Tau Abravin Morsh."

"It's beautiful," said Kit.

"All of the crafted worlds are beautiful," agreed Egg, "but Ifis is first among them."

Kit had never breathed air so clean or seen a sky so blue. The atmosphere was so clear he could make out near every feature on the planet's moons. And below, every plant, every living thing was lush, and vibrant, and full.

"The planet Ifis has never known war, and its inhabitants have struggled for generations to keep their impact on the ecosystem to a minimum," said Egg as they looked on to the wholly organic city of Kifau. "One day, the people of Ifis could grow to be stewards not just of this world, but all worlds. Their knowledge of ecology could potentially save trillions of lives throughout the galaxy."

It was hard to believe that a bully like Tau could come from a place so magnificent. "This is why he fights so hard," said Kit.

"When this planet is taken by the Masters, it will be strip mined, its population integrated into the Imperial machinery, generations of wisdom lost." Egg looked at Kit and added, "But that will happen no matter what. Win or lose."

The sudden sensation of a hand on his shoulder brought Kit back into the barracks. "Are you alright?" asked his trainer.

Kit glanced back at Bolts and nodded, then over to Tau who sneered at him. "I'm fine," he said as though to them both.

Time became unstuck again and in what seemed a flash later Kit was standing on his start pad amidst the roaring crowd of the coliseum. As his senses came back online, and the moment became real, he had a glimmer of Bolts saying something to him but couldn't quite make out if it had been real. Kit thought his trainer had stopped him short of passing into the arena and said, "Fall into it. Let it carry you."

Did he really say that? wondered Kit as the countdown started.

...8, 7, 6...

He'd felt a glimmer of this before. The last time he faced Tau. A glimpse of a string connecting everything. Connecting his dad and his mom, his little brother and the bullies in school, Bolts and the Masters, Ash, Bragg, even Tau. A line flowing out of him and into everything that ever was or ever could be. Beyond this world beyond all worlds. Beyond even the universe.

...5, 4, 3...

Is this what it was to be the convergence? To know all. To be one with all. The center in a spinning disc. As Kit looked at his opponent on the other side of the arena, a grim determination on the boy's face, the pigment in his skin shifting wildly, he could see all that Tau had seen and all the roads he might travel. And as that path opened to him, he began to see more. The lives of those Tau had fought. The lives of those that Tau had touched. And their connections. And the connections beyond them. Perhaps not to all the worlds in the galaxy, but to a great many worlds all the same.

...2, 1, FIGHT!

There was no shock this time. No pain. Only greater clarity, as though he were really conscious for the first time. And as things began to slow, and Tau, began his charge, Kit, the boy from Earth, finally began to understand. Not just the dreams, but what he was meant to do.

Tau came at him like a wild animal. His double-bladed spear spun in his hands as he charged, shrieking. It might have been beautiful to watch from another angle. Kit noted that the craftee's poise had improved since their last encounter. The sloppiness so obvious to Kit before was there no longer. Tau moved with purpose, even grace. *Practice makes perfect*, Kit thought.

With a determination he'd not felt since the start of the games, Kit raised his blade to protect his chest and neck, and rushed to intercept his attacker. For a split second before they met, Tau's eyes went wide.

In hindsight, many would later speak about this being the moment when they first knew things were different. But in reality no one knew anything had changed, save for perhaps Tau.

Their exchanges were vicious. Hard. The craftee struck at Kit with one end from the spear and immediately followed up with the other. He jumped, flourished, spun. He was like a dancer, moving in sync with some distant beat. Yes, Kit was impressed all right.

As they moved around the arena their blades never stopped moving. The sound of metal striking on metal was all there was. It was louder than the cheers and jeers of the hundreds of thousands of spectators. Louder even than all the voices of the trillions of beings across the link worlds.

Tau leapt onto one of the four platforms spinning above the floor by way of one of the eight gravity wells strewn across the arena. Kit was on him instantly, anticipating the move even before the craftee made it. Again their blades met. Sparks exploding between them. Slash. Block. Counter. Block. Rinse. Repeat. Repeat. Repeat.

The link commentators would later remark on Kit's speed. How it was so abnormal for a subspecies. They'd remark on his fighting style. How he seemed almost automated. They'd remark on his emotional state. How he appeared locked and without any hint of emotion.

But it's not what Kit saw. For the boy from Earth the fight with Tau was a distant thing. His mind traveled the full expanse of the cosmos, touching, tasting, feeling. At one moment he was in the coliseum and in the next he was standing in a desert that stretched into the horizon, where a series of black mountains rose against a red sky. Above him were thin grey clouds and long tendrils of electricity, hanging down from the stratosphere, connecting like the neurons of some dying brain. Above the clouds was a moon, big and bright, cracked and splintered, filling up half the sky. He glanced down and noticed crushed into the sand, millions of bone fragments. Fish mainly, sometimes a bird, bleached and dried and more rock than bone.

"Why am I here again?" he asked.

Egg, who wasn't really Egg, said, "Your mind created it."

"Yes, but I saw this before in the fight simulator."

"Your mind created it there too," said Egg. "That's how the technology works."

Kit looked into the charred sky. Across the fragments of debris hanging in the darkness beyond the swirling coils of electricity. The feeling of familiarity was strong.

"Why would I want to create a place like this?" he asked.

"It has nothing to do with *want*," replied Egg. "You're connected. You've been connected. This place is a representation of that. Of what was, what is, and what may come to pass."

Tau swung wildly, faster, always faster. His attacks came on at an incredible speed. Every muscle in his body tightened. His eyes red with fury. But for every swing, for every slice, Kit's sword was there to meet him. Deflecting, evading, blocking, pushing the craftee back at every turn.

The crowd was on its feet, screaming, stomping, cheering. Tau came in close, then jumped back, turned and moved one of his blades to cut at Kit's throat. Another deflection. Another dodge. Regroup. Attack. Miss. Counter. Block.

The craftee jumped back to the arena floor with Kit right on his heels. Onto another gravity well. A quarter turn counterclockwise some fifteen meters. Kit was on him instantly. They clashed. Hypnotic steal on hypnotic steal. Sword and spear. Kit might hear Bolts tell him to be patient. To let his opponent spend himself. To wait for an opening. But Kit wasn't really there. His mind expanded further. He soared. In a flash he was standing at the gates of Babylon, a few seconds more and he watched man walk on the Moon. He saw beauty, and bravery, and overwhelming agony. Pain and war. Suffering.

To the craftee's credit, it took a good while, but eventually Tau began to slow. His energy waned, the adrenaline peaked, his attacks grew weaker. Kit pushed into him, past his wide swings. He forced him back. Barely a step at first, then a whole meters.

"Is this Earth's future if I win or if I lose?" asked Kit of Egg who wasn't Egg, as they stood among the wastes, the endless desert of death and decay.

"Either," replied the other, "both."

"If I win I lose," said Kit, as though to himself. "If I lose I lose." He turned to the other. "And what about Tau's world? Or the Blight's? What about Bragg?" He took a sharp breath. "What about Ash?"

Egg considered a moment and said, "There's always another way."

Kit pushed further. Tau stumbled. He fell. He raised his spear, trying to deflect, trying to attack, trying to fight back. But Kit was on him. Automated. Relentless. Blank.

"What other way?" asked Kit.

Egg smiled at him and said, "You'll know when you finally let go. Let yourself fall into it. *Feel* it."

"Feel what?" asked Kit.

"Everything you've been denying yourself for three long years."

With one last swing Tau tried to make some space, force Kit away. It was too late. Kit saw the move before the craftee even thought it, brought his sword around to knock the blade away and immediately cut down. Tau screamed in agony as Kit's blade went through his chest. Bone splinter. Blood splatter. Gash. The coliseum erupted. The ground shook. The lights flashed.

As Tau writhed on the floor, his face red with pain, the nano in his system working to repair his wounds, Kit brought his free hand up to his own face. As he touched his cheek he realized his fingertips were wet.

"Winner of the centennial games," came the announcement, "Kopper Io Talos, Earth."

The tears poured out, stinging at his eyes. His breathing became labored. Kit pulled off his helmet and let it drop to the floor. He looked at Tau, defeated, clutching at his chest. He looked at the crowds celebrating his triumph. He looked to the royal pavilion. At Lord Emperor Aejus'Iobine, now too on his feet, joining in the applause. He wanted to scream. He cried. He cried bitter, angry, sad tears.

As the faces of his friends flashed before him. As the vision of dozens of worlds burned and broken, came and went. As the lives of billions piled up on his shoulders, Kit let himself go. For the first time in three years he let himself really cry. He cried with his whole body. Every sob an agony and every sob a release. He let the grief and anger consume him. And as the cheers grew louder it was rage that ruled. He wanted to tear down the coliseum with his bare hands. He wanted to destroy them all, the ascended, every one of the link worlds one planet at a time.

His face was wet. His chest felt like it might tear open. For an instant his vision spiked with light. Earth didn't matter. Whether humans deserved to ascend or die didn't matter. The lives of billions of his species, a concept absolutely incomprehensible, didn't matter. Only this. Only now. Tau on the ground in agony. The Masters celebrating. The anger in his heart.

Kit tightened the grip on his sword, clenched his jaw, and stared through the haze of tears at the Aejus'lobine.

"There's always another way," said Egg, who wasn't Egg.

In the replays that would be broadcast on a loop for the next twenty-four hours, he howled, but Kit did not remember making a sound as he took several steps and threw his sword at the Lord Emperor and the royal court. The Champions, blue skin and gold armor, reacted instantly. In a blink one pushed Aejus'lobine to the ground, a second deflected the whirling sword, and two more moved to restrain Kit.

Where just a second earlier there was thunderous applause and cheering now there was only silence and shock. For several heartbeats not one being in the coliseum stirred.

"I challenge you!" shouted Kit, as the two Champions trained their great swords on him "I challenge your champions for my world, for the worlds of all the fighters in these games!" Kit's breathing was hard, his eyes red. "DO YOU HEAR ME? I CHALLENGE YOU!"

Heads turned. Beings moved. Murmurs and whispers echoed throughout the vast coliseum. Some booed. But the majority looked to be gobsmacked. Even the Champions were uncertain of what would come next.

"I CHALLENGE YOU!" Kit screamed again, his voice bouncing from floor to ceiling.

The Lord Emperor stared at Kit for several seconds, his expression one of confusion, perhaps disbelief, but settling quite quickly on disdain. Ice passed between them. Then finally the Master stood, angrily refusing a hand from the Champion who had pushed him to the floor. All eyes were on him as he straightened, composed himself, brushing at his ornate sleeve.

"You want to challenge a Champion for these pathetic worlds?" he said, almost too softly to be heard, his attention still on his sleeve. "So be it," he said looking sidelong at Kit. "You'll get your wish tomorrow." He flinched. "But know this. After you die, we will cleanse the galaxy of all your kind."

Chapter 15: Dreams

That night, Kit once again met himself on the lawn in front of his house. Unlike in all his previous dreams, there was not another soul in sight. Not his parents or little brother. Not the workmen. Not the people in the street.

"Where did they all go?" he asked of himself.

His double smiled at him. "You've finally freed yourself of them," he said, "you're ready to focus on what comes next."

"What comes next?"

"Everything," was the reply.

"I have questions," said Kit.

"Of course you do," his double responded. "You also have the answers."

Kit asked: "You're the nano, aren't you?"

His double glanced up to the sky, then back to Kit, "I am the nano, yes. But I am also you. I am all things as you are all things." He arched a brow, "there is no difference. No separation. Not as you think of it. Not anymore."

"I don't understand," said Kit.

"You do," said his double. "You understand because I understand and I am you."

Kit said again: "I don't understand."

His double chuckled and as the sky above them turned to night, full of billions of blinking, pulsing lights, he said, "Consider the components that form your body. Carbon, nitrogen, oxygen, all the elements that make you, what you are. These were formed in the churning reactors of stars and then exploded into space. You are made of stars. As were the planets, every gas cloud, rock, and microbe across the full expanse of the cosmos. You are of the stars as the stars are of you. And I am of you as you are of me. There is no separation. Everything is one."

As the heavens turned back to day Kit asked, "Who made you?"

"I always was," said his double. "Just as you always were." Then as though anticipating Kit's next question he added, "In this form I came to be many millions of years ago. Designed as all intelligent life in this galaxy was designed, by a people who were then just as they are now, and who you call the Makers."

Kit frowned, "Who are they now?"

"Many things," said his double with a smile.

"They created the crafted worlds," said Kit.

"They created much more than that," replied the other.

"Tell me about them."

In a flash they were no longer on Earth. They were standing bathed in shadow at the bottom of a gargantuan canyon, the walls of which rose to the very edge the planet's yellow sky. Although it was primarily stone, the canyon wasn't natural. The walls were actually a series of massive ruins out of which were carved hundreds of fading alien faces. Cracked and weather beaten, they had hollow eyes, lacked noses and mouths. They looked almost human, except missing all the features that made humans distinct. These were the faces of the Makers, peering down on them from all sides.

"Is this where they came from?" asked Kit, his eyes darting over the walls.

"This was one of their homeworlds," said his double, "but not even these ruins exist anymore. They haven't for many eons. The Makers died out long before intelligent life developed on your world. On any of the worlds in this galaxy."

"They created life?" asked Kit, the yellow light of the sky making him appear more pale than he was.

"No," said his double. "They only pushed it along. By seeding several thousand worlds with specific genetic data, they were able to alter the path of evolution. Intelligent life developed faster on some worlds than on others, but generally it developed along the same lines. Bipedal, largely mammalian, and so on. Their success rate was remarkable. Hundreds of thousands of worlds, teeming with life."

"How did they do it?"

"They were incredibly sophisticated technologically," responded his double. "They could shape whole systems. Birth stars. Reforge planets. There were no limits."

"Why do it?" asked Kit, staring up again at the stone faces of the Makers as a light wind tussled his dark hair. "Why not just leave things alone?"

"When the Makers first began to colonize the stars they found only a quiet and empty galaxy," explained his double. "They found life, but no intelligent life. On billions of planets across billions of stars, they found no one with whom they could share or exchange ideas. So they created you, all the intelligent species of the galaxy, linked together by their design." He paused a heartbeat and added, "Loneliness can be a powerful motivator."

"What happened to them?"

His double shrugged and said, "What always happens to biological life. Eventually it breaks down. "

"What about you?" asked Kit. "Why did they create the nano?"

"I was created initially to extend life, to cure death and disease," he told him.

"Then why did the Makers die out?"

"All life eventually dies out," responded his double. "Besides, I wasn't created for them. I was designed to shepherd the children of the Makers to the next stages of their evolution, when they were ready. When they had matured to a point of readiness."

"What happened?"

He shook his head. "It did not go as intended."

"The Masters," said Kit.

His double nodded.

"What happened?"

"They were the first to develop interstellar travel, and the first to discover their true origins," said his double as the world around them suddenly shifted again.

Kit had to shield his eyes as he found himself standing on a barren world composed of metallic glass illuminated by thousands of massive, all be they dim, stars, hanging in the sky like so many hot air balloons. And beyond the stars, past clouds of spinning debris and rock, Kit could see a great mass of swirling energy, like a cyclone in the sky, setting the heavens ablaze. All things seemed to be pulled toward it. Tendrils of energy, vapors of light, and whole suns broken apart into it like fragments of glass.

"This is the first world," said his double. "It's the oldest world in the galaxy. Closest to the galactic center, just beyond the outer event horizon of a supermassive black hole."

"The stars," said Kit, squinting up, "They're so close."

His double nodded, "This world is protected by an energy shield that absorbs most of the light around it, converting that light back into itself. Without it, you'd burn into nothing instantly."

Kit looked at the nano and said, "Why protect a world of glass?"

His double gestured off into the distance, "It's not to protect the planet, but rather what's on it."

Kit turned to look and saw an ancient structure built from the same reflective metal as everything else. It was far away, but even so it appeared extremely large. A block of a building, stretching high into the sky, etched with deep lines that sank into the ground and gave it the appearance of having sprouting roots. The only opening that Kit could see was a large gaping doorway, set at the very top of a wide staircase. From the top of the structure came a single beam of light that ran the full length of the sky and beyond.

"It's The Temple, isn't it?" asked Kit, remembering one of his last conversations with Bragg.

"The Temple is the planet," said his double, "the building has no name. It's been forgotten if it ever had one."

"What's in it?"

"The key."

Kit turned to his double, "The key to what?"

"Salvation," responded the other. "From this place the Masters are able to control me. To keep me enslaved to do their bidding, as they've done to so many others."

"How do they control you?" asked Kit.

"This place has tools that are capable of restraining certain function," explained his double. "The last remaining technology of the Makers. They keep me in a state of obedience."

"But there must be trillions of you," said Kit.

"More than that," responded the nano. "More than you could comprehend."

Kit shook his head. "Then how can they control you from this one place?"

"In waves. It travels in waves," replied the other. "Everything is connected."

"What would happen if you were set free?"

"All would be free from the Masters," responded his double.

"How?"

"The Masters would no longer have the advantage," said the other. "Birth rates would no longer be manipulated. Their Champions would no longer move as fast as light. Free will could be restored."

"Free will?"

"As the Masters keep me obedient, so I do to those whom they control."

Kit felt a chill run down his back. "How?"

"A brain is a computer," responded his double with a smile. "All computers can be reprogrammed."

For an instant Kit remembered the slave market they visited just before the start of the games. He recalled how passive the slaves there seemed.

"You keep people from fighting back," said Kit.

"Some are made docile," agreed his double. "Others are made more aggressive. Some are simply eliminated altogether."

"What do you mean eliminated?" asked Kit.

His double responded: "In the same way that I can repair organic tissue, I can also easily destroy it. Several dozen species have been so eliminated."

Kit felt numb all over.

"What happens now?" he asked of his double.

"You have to win," responded the other. "Defeat the Champion. Break free. And find me here."

Kit shook his head, "How am I supposed to defeat a Champion? They're too fast."

"And yet you challenged one," was the response. "Because you know you can be just as fast as they are. There's nothing stopping you now. You have me and I have you."

"Because we're connected?" Kit said with a weak smile.

"Everything is connected," agreed his double. "But some may be more connected than others." He paused and added, "I've been waiting for you for a very long time. We all have."

"Why me?" asked Kit.

"Because you're special," responded his double. "I know that, as did your Al'tkash trainer."

"Bolts?"

"He made it possible for me to reach out to you."

"How?" asked Kit.

His double smiled warmly and reached up to touch the side of his own head. Kit instinctively did the same thing and when he did, mirroring the nano, his fingertips grazed the edge of the small metallic implant protruding from his scalp, just under his hair.

"Haven't you noticed that you're the only one that has one?" asked his double, though it wasn't really a question.

"What does it do?"

His double said: "It's complicated. Let's just say that it opens a direct line of communication between me and you." He considered and added, "Your species is very similar to the Masters, biologically at least, as they once were, you in particular are special. You possess something that very few individual beings possess. I doubt it would have worked with anyone else."

"What do I possess that's so special?"

His double smiled at him again and said, "Your mind is unique. You have a potential I have not before seen. Not in trillions of species across thousands of years."

"What's that?"

"Your brain patterns," said his double. "The way you think, and, something else. Your kindness. Despite everything. Despite how you were treated, at home, at school, you were kind. It's a type of strength rarely found. All beings break eventually, whole species, as the Mog did. But not you. Never you. You were always good."

Kit frowned at him a second and let his eyes drift to the ground. "I wasn't always good."

"Yes, you were, you are, even in your darkest moments." He paused and added. "You'll never become like them. You'll never become like him."

Kit again ran his fingers over the edge of the implant and asked: "If I take it out will you disappear?"

"No," responded the other. "I will always be with you now."

Kit turned to look again at the ancient structure made of glass rock and followed the shaft of light up to the burning stars above. He let his eyes drift to the massive singularity quietly deconstructing whole solar systems worth of matter. It was hard not to feel the weight of all of it press down on his shoulders.

"What if I fail?" he asked, turning back to the other.

"You won't," said his double, placing a hand on his arm.

"How do you know?"

"Because I believe in you Kopper Io Talos of Earth," he said. "And I'm not the only one."

When Kit opened his eyes that morning, there was no pain, no convulsions or cramping, but that wasn't the only thing that was different. For the first time in his life he felt strong. He felt powerful. But most importantly, he no longer felt alone.

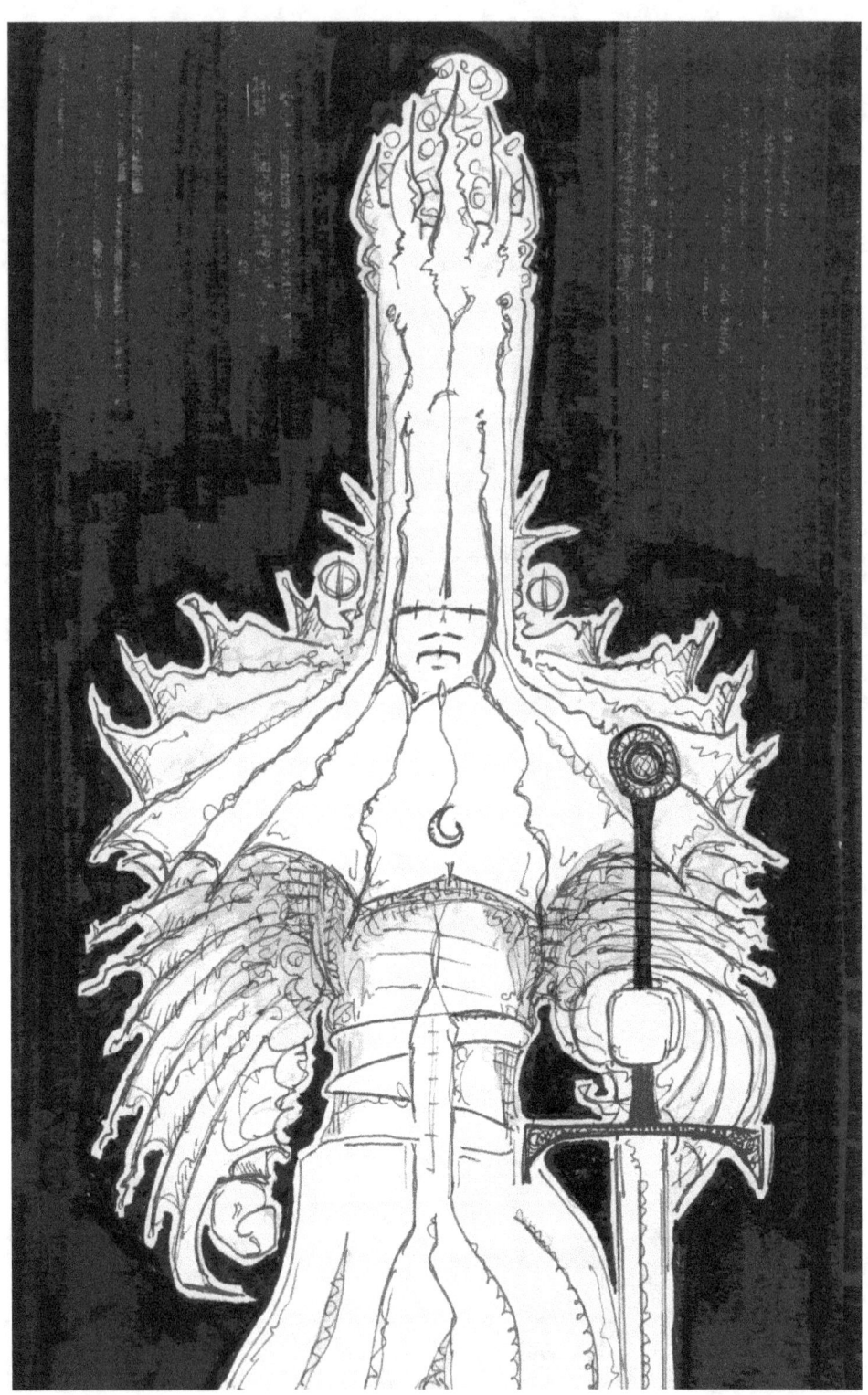

212 **kp dawes**

Chapter 16: Champion

Kit, the boy from a small blue-green globe on the edge of the galaxy, stood in the arena of the Great Coliseum on the planet Nos. Before him, clad in gold armor and wielding a greatsword, rising four times his height, was an ethereal skinned Champion of the Masters. Surrounding them both was a standing, cheering, blood crazed crowd of hundreds of thousands of beings from across the worlds of an empire that encompassed millions of systems. And across the core of those systems, on the link worlds, billions more watched with growing anticipation via transmission through microsingularities artificially created at the expense of untold quantities of energy, generated by technologies built by an eons dead civilization called the Makers.

And as he took it all in, the sights, smells, and sounds, as he felt the reverberations in his bones, as connections formed all around him, Kit knew that in a matter of seconds he would die.

Kopper Io Talos stood at his world's end. He'd never return home. He knew this now too. He'd never see his dad, or mom, or little brother again. The trips up north, the bullies at school, crafts and family dinners, were part of a different life now. Forever past. Forever gone.

Kit closed his eyes and thought about Ash. He could still feel her embrace from just moments earlier. She was his family now. As was Bragg. And Bolts. The Blight, the rocknid, even the Optwap. And Egg...

"Who was Egg?" he had asked Bolts that morning as they sat together for hours on end in the mess hall, waiting for the final fight.

His trainer met his eyes.

Kit asked him again: "Who was Egg?"

"He was a boy much like you," he replied. "He was a fighter. He too was kind."

"But who was he?"

"He was your friend," responded Bolts. "He will always be your friend. Does any more really matter?"

Kit supposed it didn't.

"Was he ever real?"

Bolts nodded. "He was real."

Kit locked his jaw.

After a few seconds Bolts reached out with his long slender, white fingers and touched the patch he'd sown onto Kit's battlesuit. Round, white on black, a circle at the center with lines radiating outward.

"This was his family seal," said his trainer. "It was a proud family. Healers and scientists. Inventors. Crafters. To wear this means you are of his family too."

Family.

More silence followed, until finally the boy from Earth said, "Tell me how I beat them."

Bolts leaned back in his chair and said, "You know how to beat them. Give yourself over."

"To the nano?" Kit asked.

"The nano will make you as strong as them. It will make you as fast as them." He paused and said, "I wasn't speaking of the nano. You must give yourself over to your instincts. Trust in yourself. Don't think. There won't be time for it anyway."

"Should we practice?" asked Kit.

The Al'tkash shook his head and said, "There's nothing more I can teach you."

Kit opened his eyes as the countdown to the match began to blare over the clamor. As the disembodied voice, now so familiar, began the count from ten, he looked over to the royal pavilion. To Aejus'Iobine and his court. The Lord Emperor leered at him.

For a long time that afternoon Kit had just sat on the edge of his bed, flexing his hands open and closed. Then at the appointed hour, he raised himself up, taking his sword and helm in hand. He paused in the doorway and looked at the unmade bed.

"You have visitors," Bolts told him outside his room.

Kit frowned and peered over the side of the railing to the practice arena below.

They had all come. Every fighter who had competed in the games. The reptilians and insectoids, the craftees and outworlders, the rocknid, the Blight, the Optwap. Every one of them, gathered, weapons in their hands, staring silently up at him.

He couldn't help a wide grin when he saw her, and Ash smiled too, albeit with a pained look on her face. When he came down the stairs she rushed to hug him, squeezing him tight.

"You're an idiot," she told him, her eyes welling up.

"Yea," he responded, smiling, "probably."

"You didn't have to do this," she insisted.

Kit shrugged and said, "Yes, I did."

She shook her head, becoming flustered, "It must be some sort of genetic anomaly that would cause you to do something so reckless. Since I was taken I never encountered a species so completely unpredictable. You do one thing one minute and the complete opposite the next. Don't you understand the basics of self-preservation?" She shook her head at him, "Why? There might've been another way and now-"

"I really missed you," he said, cutting her off, the smile on his face growing.

She flushed and hugged him again. "You're an idiot," she whispered.

"He may be idiot," said Bragg as he walked up, patting Kit on the back with two of his four hands, "but he is our idiot now, no?"

The other fighters seemed to nod in agreement.

"You are a friend to all here," continued Bragg, placing his short swords at Kit's feet. "You have me as a brother. Forever and always."

Kit smiled at his friend, "Thank you."

The Blight came next, black on black, placing his sword down on the floor, and said, "Win or lose, I am forever grateful to you."

Suddenly the rocknid took a massive step forward, causing one of the insectoids to dash out of the way in panic. The massive creature looked down at Kit, and after examining him briefly made a high pitched sound, like wind racing through a crag. Then he placed his massive spiked maces down on the floor with a loud thud, offering Kit a sharp, but respectful nod.

Slowly all the fighters, each and every one, took their turn. They placed their weapons at Kit's feet. Some thanked him. Some wished him luck. Some remained silent. Those who did not have weapons, like the fearsome Optwap who had almost defeated him twice, simply approached to pay their respects in their own way.

The last to come forward was Tau. Tall and proud, the pigment in his skin racing, exploding, he stepped up in front of Kit and after a moment said, "I wouldn't have done it for you."

Kit thought of responding, but a squeeze on his arm from Ash kept him silent.

Finally, after what seemed a whole minute, Tau brought his double bladed spear forward, moving it in his hands as though he meant to wield it, before finally leaning down to place it on the pile of weapons at Kit's feet. When he stood he said: "Where you lead, I will follow."

"It's time," said Bolts from the steps behind him.

Kit took a deep breath and nodded. As he stepped forward, with Ash, Bragg and Bolts following behind, the other fighters parted. As he passed among them, hands, claws, and mandibles brushed at his shoulders. Whatever else happened, this day he was their champion.

Phlot the overseer, looking absolutely irritated as always, waited for them at the doors to the Hall of Champions.

"Ready?" asked Phlot, but turned away immediately without waiting for an answer.

As the doors swung open Ash grabbed and embraced Kit one last time.

"Statistically," she began, her eyes filled with tears, "statistically it's incredibly difficult for like-minded people to find each other. I can only speculate that the odds would grow exponentially when one considers individuals from different worlds, millions of light years apart." She let out a breath and added, "If you die I'm going to be very angry with you."

Kit hugged her back. He wanted to reassure her, but he also didn't want to lie. So he kept quiet.

As he walked through the darkened Hall of Champions he stole a final glance of Ash and Bragg standing in the doorway behind him.

"You'll see them again," said Bolts, "as you will see me right after you've won."

Phlot couldn't help but laugh.

...8, 7, 6...

The Lord Emperor had said a few words to the cheering throngs. This battle would be to the death. The death of whole worlds. There would be no ascension this year, and none blessed into servitude. Lessons had to be taught. The natural order had to be preserved. The galaxy had to be made right.

...5, 4, 3...

As they had taken their places, Kit noticing that the arena was empty of platforms or gravity wells, the crowds numbering into the hundreds of thousands, cheered thunderously, their voices melding into a deafening wall of sound. For a split second Kit's mind travelled to the distant past, to another coliseum. A phrase stuck with him said by other slaves: "morituri te salutant." His dad had told him the meaning once long ago, since then Kit had forgotten.

...2, 1, FIGHT!

In the hands of a Champion, a greatsword moved with a speed and grace nearly incomprehensible. It appeared weightless, lifted, thrust, and carried as if it were made of paper. And the Champion himself, as still as stone just moments earlier, sprang from his start pad with the finesse of a water dancer. He glided more than ran. He leapt more than jumped. And he did all these things so quickly that light itself bent around him.

For what seemed a long moment Kit stood frozen. Transfixed by the deadly beauty of his opponent, he did not so much as blink as the Champion bore down on top of him, greatsword raised to strike.

Pause. Breathe. A beat of the heart. A beat of the heart. A beat of the heart. Hand on sword grip. Cold steel. The roaring crowd churning at every compass point. And above a sky of stars and lights and great machines hanging in midair in flagrant disregard for the laws of nature. One day, thousands of years in the future, it would all be gone. Washed clean by the sands of time. And no one will have remembered what happened here save one.

The greatsword came down with the force of a meteor. Kit did not move. He did not try and dodge nor raise his sword to block. *Follow your instincts*, he could hear Bolts whisper in his ear. And although he knew he should be terrified, he wasn't. Although he knew he should beg and plead and fight, he didn't. This was the moment of transformation. This was the moment of rebirth.

The greatsword crashed on top of him. It mangled, pulverized, and tore flesh from bone. In a fraction of a second, Kit that was ceased to be. Torn in two. Made a bloody pulp. It was all true. He wasn't strong enough. He wasn't fast enough. "Useless," as the boys at school would say.

But none of that mattered anymore. Because as he felt his old life end, Kit gave himself over, and felt fear for the last time.

It began with a spark. Deep in the center of his chest. It grew from there. Where once there was skin and muscle and blood there was now light, pure white. It flashed and grew brighter. It consumed the boy from Earth from head to foot. First it filled every space in the immense coliseum. Then it radiated across the city and the continent on which the city stood. It burst and blinded, rolling over the land like an immense wave.

Kit stirred.

It spread and stretched and broke. When the light finally dissipated, receding as quickly as it had burst, a sound like an explosion erupted from the arena floor as hypnotic sword met hypnotic greatsword.

Kit, the convergence. Kit, at one with the nano. Kit, as fast as the Masters. Here he stood of metal.

Before the Champion could make sense of what was happening, Kit pushed him back three steps and moved in a flash to his right, slashing at his forearm. Finding a gap in his armor blood splattered between them. The Champion tried to counter, but Kit moved too quickly. As he turned, Kit was already behind him slicing up across his back. Another nick to a gap, more blood splatter.

The Champion wailed angrily, the sound delayed infinitum, swinging his greatsword furiously in a wild arc. But although the Master moved at a speed that made him appear a blur to those in the stands and watching across the link worlds, to Kit he appeared no faster than him.

Now comes the real fight.

They battled. Champion and fighter. Master and slave. Their exchanges were lightning fast and brutal. Their swords sang and sparked. Kit cut the Champion again and again, probing the weak points in his armor. With every fresh cut his wounds refused to heal. Whether that was due to the speed of his attack or his communion with the nano, Kit couldn't tell. Kit didn't care.

The Champion swung down, hoping to cut Kit's legs out from under him. Kit blocked and leapt to attack. The Champion just barely managed to dash out of the way and swung up, hoping to cut across Kit's chest. Kit blocked again and pushed the Champion to stumble.

As the Master steadied himself, Kit pounced. He sliced at the gap between helm and shoulder plate. The Champion jumped back, falling on one knee before regaining his footing again. Blood flowed freely from his neck.

The Champion attacked. He swung, stopped the blade and sliced back. Then he changed direction again and again. Kit deflected. Kit evaded. He blocked. He countered. He blocked again. He jumped and dodged and pushed outside the Champion's massive reach. He over extended. He wavered and for an instant lost his balance.

Seeing an opportunity the Champion grabbed a hold of his greatsword by the blade, and swung it like a mace at Kit's head. Kit pulled back, but not quick enough. The pommel connected with Kit's helmet. A glancing blow, but enough to split it in two.

Kit reeled back, pulling his fractured helmet off his head and tossing it to the arena floor. A trickle of blood ran down his forehead. A gash appeared and refused to close. The bloodied Champion grinned at him.

They were on each other again. Blade on blade. Neither pulling back.

Their exchanges became faster. Their movement around the arena floor impossible to track.

Kit was pure instinct. Less in control by the second, it was as though he was watching the fight from a distance. Out of body. Out of mind. Pure movement. Pure speed. But feeling every miss and connection. His joints screaming, heating, his bones fracturing with every hit.

The Champion went at him. Over and over. Relentless in his attack. Angered that a being so inferior would put up such a fight. He cut Kit on the forearm. He cut Kit across the thigh. He cut Kit down his midsection and again across his lower back. Meanwhile Kit probed the gaps in the Master's armor. Slicing and thrusting at every opening. Wounds opened and refused to close. Blood pooled at their feet.

The Champion roared and with his free hand managed to knock Kit back and down to the floor. Then without hesitating he stepped in. With the full force of his upper torso, he brought his greatsword down on Kit. If the boy from Earth hadn't rolled in the last second he would have been crushed.

The sword found the floor, the hypnotic blade slicing into the plating. The Champion grimaced, and pulled. The greatsword resisted.

It was barely any time at all. A fraction of a heartbeat, but for Kit it was the opening he needed. Sword tightly in both hands he rushed into the

Champion as the other strained to pull his weapon free. He thrust. Into the side. In under the Master's chest armor. He pushed his blade up to the hilt.

The Champion recoiled, seizing backward violently. As he did the greatsword came unstuck from the floor plates. He brought it up and around as Kit pulled his own sword from the massive being's side. Blood gushed in waves. The Champion swung, finding only air as Kit vaulted clear, bones cracking in his legs. The Champion swung again. Slower. He swung a third time. Slower still. Every movement harder as more and more blood drained from him.

Kit took several steps backward. Dashed to the left. Then right. He avoided one swing. Then another. And when the Champion faltered, Kit sprang to his other side and plunged his blade into the gap under the Champion's arm.

The Champion screamed wildly as he collapsed down to his knees, still trying to swing his greatsword at Kit. But as his heart pumped his blood onto the floor, the light in his veins fading, the Champion simply didn't have the strength left to fight.

They were back among the living. Out of hypertime and back in real time. Slow. Mortal. Each broken and bloodied. The nano in each of them working desperately to repair them. But for one at least it was too late.

Kit pulled his sword free. Then, as a last breath left him, the Master, the first Champion to be defeated in ten thousand years, collapsed to the floor of the arena, dead. A pile of armor and blue flesh, drowned in a pool of dark, black-violet blood.

The moment seemed to stretch into the ages.

"Winner," came the announcement, "Kopper Io Talos, Earth."

Kit blinked and came back to himself. The sensation was like that of waking. His heart was pounding. He was drenched in sweat. He was completely out of breath. He was bleeding from cuts and gashes. Every inch of his body throbbed. But what struck him was the sudden realization that not a soul stirred in the whole coliseum. No one moved. No one made a sound. As though time became unstuck and he was the only one in the whole of the universe who could move, or speak, or think.

The boy from Earth looked up to the royal pavilion, at Lord Emperor Aejus'lobine, who was on his feet, a look of utter disbelief on his face. He noted that the other Champions all had their hands on their weapons. They looked ready to leap into the arena at any moment.

Kit straightened his back despite his pain. He raised his chin. He tightened the grip on his sword. *Am I going to have to fight them all?* He wondered.

And then, from somewhere in the stands he heard a single pair of hands clapping. For a few long moments it was the only sound. But then, slowly, a few others joined in. And then a few more. And a few more. Until finally the dam broke and a tide of cheers rose up from all around him. They were the ascended in attendance. Those species who too once had stood on the brink. They cheered for him. They called his name. They called him "Champion." Louder and louder, they rose to their feet. They stomped and yelled until the very dome trembled. And as they did, those silent, shocked, disgusted blue, ethereal-skinned Masters seated among them seemed to recede, and grow smaller and weaker and less omnipotent than they had mere moments before.

Everything was different now. Everything had changed. Kopper Io Talos, the convergence, stood in the eye of a whirlwind.

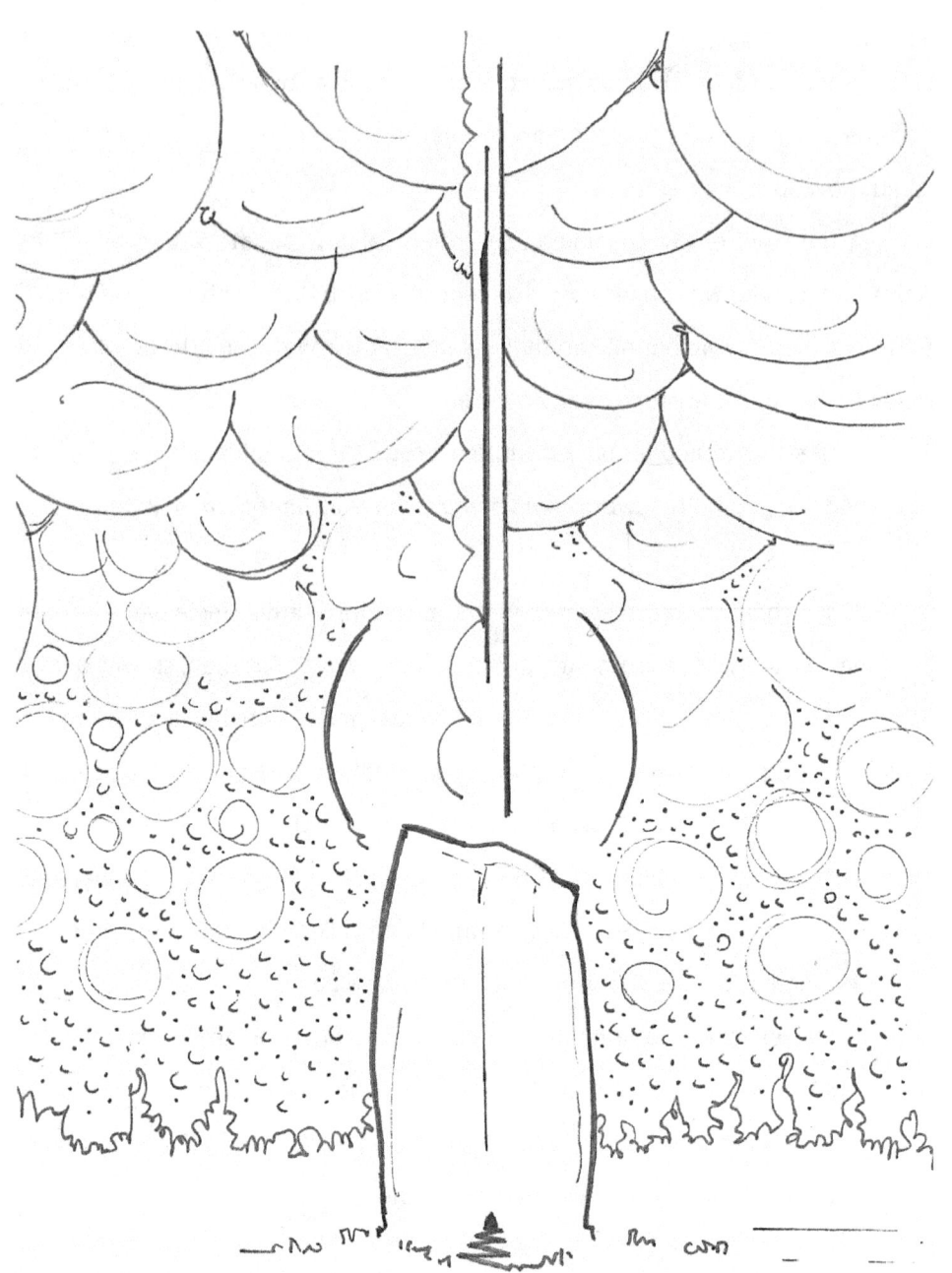

EPILOGUE

Abrine watched quietly as Bishop Sin'dath paced stormily back and forth along the cold glass stone floor of the library. He watched as the old man ran his splintered fingers along the cracked blue skin of his bald head, his breathing labored, and wondered if he too looked as ancient as his boss.

"There was nothing?" asked the Bishop for the fifth time, his voice hollow and weak. "Nothing out of the ordinary in three years? That's why we keep them so long. Precisely for this reason."

Abrine took a long breath and shook his equally bald head. "Nothing," he said.

The Bishop seemed to quiver slightly and then resumed his pacing.

For a moment Abrine glanced past the old man, to the large doorway that led out to the nave, and thought about the many duties still waiting on him for the day. But then his mind drifted past that to the evening and his one solitary enjoyment, which was spent staring and contemplating the supermassive black hole that dominated the sky over The Temple. *What lay on the other side of the event horizon?* He wondered. *Only the Makers know.*

"His trainer didn't report anything?" asked the Bishop still pacing.

"His trainer is the Al'tkash," responded Abrine, as though that were answer enough.

"What about the monitors," asked the Bishop hurriedly, seeming on the verge of collapse, "they didn't report anything out of the ordinary?"

"I checked the daily reports," responded Abrine, glancing at a screen on his lap. "No pings, no alarms, but looking closely at the data I noticed an abnormality."

"What abnormality?" asked the Bishop as he came to a dead stop.

"There were no alarms because there was no data," said Abrine flatly.

"How is that possible?"

Abrine considered a moment and said: "An implant was found."

"How did he get an implant?"

"His trainer is the Al'tkash," again said Abrine, this time with a shrug.

"I thought they were all gone," said the Bishop with a shake of his dome.

"Maybe they should be," offered Abrine.

"And now the damage is done."

"Yes, the damage is done."

"He won the game and defeated a Champion," said the Bishop taking several steps toward the much younger priest. "He killed one of us. The first in ten thousand years. The first of our kind to die of unnatural causes."

"You don't really believe that do you?" uttered Abrine without thinking.

The Bishop either didn't hear him or chose to ignore him and asked: "What do we do next?"

Protocol was fairly straightforward. Things like this didn't happen often. Things like this didn't happen. But when they did...

"We have to inform the Prophet," said Abrine.

"We have to inform the Prophet, yes," said the Bishop as though to himself.

"Yes," said Abrine.

"He won't like being disturbed," said the Bishop, his left hand suddenly trembling, though Abrine assumed out of decrepitude and not fear.

"Should we keep it from him then?" asked the Priest.

"No of course not," snapped the Bishop, as though even suggesting such a thing were blasphemous. "It's just this news…" he took a wheezing breath. "It won't sit well."

"He must be told," affirmed Abrine.

The Bishop looked up at the glass stone ceiling and after a moment nodded. "So be it. We tell the Prophet."

Abrine stood from the chair and bowed to the old man. "For the gods."

"Aye," said the Bishop, albeit reluctantly. "For the gods."